GUILT
GAME

ALSO BY L.J. SELLERS

The Detective Jackson Series

The Sex Club
Secrets to Die For
Thrilled to Death
Passions of the Dead
Dying for Justice
Liars, Cheaters & Thieves
Rules of Crime
Crimes of Memory
Deadly Bonds
Wrongful Death
Death Deserved

The Agent Dallas Series

The Trigger
The Target
The Trap

Stand-Alone Novels

The Gender Experiment
Point of Control
The Lethal Effect (previously published as *The Suicide Effect*)
The Baby Thief
The Gauntlet Assassin

GUILT GAME

L.J. SELLERS

THOMAS & MERCER

Published by Thomas & Mercer, Seattle
www.apub.com

Amazon, the Amazon logo, and Thomas & Mercer are trademarks of Amazon.com, Inc., or its affiliates.

ISBN-13: 9781477848395
ISBN-10: 1477848398

Cover design by Damonza

Printed in the United States of America

GUILT GAME

GUILT
GAME

CHAPTER 1

Tuesday, April 18, 9:52 a.m., Salem, Oregon

Roxanne MacFarlane watched on the monitor as three people approached the building. A bearded fifty-something man, a thin anxious woman, and a pensive teenage girl. *Damn!* The reverend had come along. This could get sticky. Rox hoped she didn't have to resort to kidnapping, but she would do whatever it took to help her client. Every case was personal for her.

The trio disappeared inside the building, so Rox glanced at the second monitor. The view of the lobby was a little distorted, but she could clearly see her partner—her stepdad, Marty, in a fake security uniform—scoot out from behind a small counter. He blocked the access door and gestured for the man in the black cloak to step aside for a weapons search. The reverend looked annoyed but complied.

That was her cue. Time to put on the act. Grabbing the girl and dragging her out would be easier, but at forty years old, Rox was finally learning to pretend. After a deep breath, she bolted down the short hall, opened the door to the lobby, and stepped partway in. "Mia Bankston? You're late for your appointment." Rox focused on the girl, a slender fourteen-year-old.

"I am? I'm sorry." Mia bit her lip and turned to her mother. The woman shrugged and glanced at the phony spiritual leader and polygamist she'd married. Reverend Jonah was arguing with the security guard, who had his hands under the cult leader's robe. *Nice touch, Marty.*

Rox stepped forward, holding the door open. "Let's get this done right now, or we'll have to reschedule. I have another appointment soon."

"I'd like to wait for my husband." The mother's voice was soft and uncertain.

"I just need Mia to sign." Rox paused, then projected her voice. "If she wants her money *today*." She had lured the girl and her mother—who rarely left the polygamist's home—with a letter about a phony inheritance.

"Go ahead," the self-appointed reverend said. "I'll be right behind you." He was pulling ID from his wallet.

Greed had overruled his usual control and caution.

The girl stepped past Rox and through the opening. Rox quickly followed and shut the door behind her, locking the mother out. Rox grabbed Mia's arm and steered her down the hall. She had rented the small building for a week just for this assignment.

"What about my mother?" The girl seemed surprised but not alarmed.

So far so good. Ideally Mia's actions should be voluntary. "Your great-aunt left the money specifically to you. I just need a signature so I can release the funds." Rox kept moving. She'd done her best to disguise herself with a wig and oversize reading glasses, but she still wanted minimal exposure. During her time at the CIA, they'd never let her do fieldwork, but she'd learned a lot from the operatives anyway.

Behind them the mother screeched, "Why is this door locked?"

The girl stopped.

Damn! Two more steps. Rox gave a small shrug. "Don't worry, it's just stuck. Happens every day, but I don't have time to deal with it right now." She tugged on Mia's arm. "Come get your money."

For a moment, the girl hesitated, her eyes wary.

Rox gave her another charming smile. She was dressed in her only lawyer-looking clothes, a navy skirt and jacket, and she knew she had a trustworthy face. One of the reasons they'd hired her at the CIA—that, and her analytical skills.

Mia shrugged and moved forward. Rox opened the door at the end of the hall, and they entered the room where her client waited.

The girl let out a shocked cry. "Dad?" She stepped forward, confusion and joy playing out on her innocent face. "I thought you were dead!"

"No, honey. No . . . I'm . . ."

They ran toward each other and embraced in a tight hug.

Rox smiled. This was why she did this work—to reunite people with their families.

The man and his daughter stepped apart and started crying. Tears of joy had always confused Rox. Why did people cry when they were supposed to be happy? It wasn't logical. But she'd become used to not being able to read people correctly. Except for Marty, who she'd had a lifetime to figure out.

Rox took a photo of the two, then stepped out of the room to give the family some privacy. Her part was done. Now it was up to her client to convince his daughter to go with him—rather than stay in the polygamous cult and end up as a child bride for a man who already had six wives and fourteen children he controlled with an iron fist. Mia's father had joint custody, which had been established at birth with his name on the certificate, and never altered in court. But Mia's mother had taken the girl and gone into hiding.

Rox was careful about custody issues and had done her homework. At fourteen, the girl was free to choose who she wanted to live with. Her client had hired her to find the girl, then get her out. He hadn't trusted the legal system to help because he had a criminal drug record. But he'd turned his life around and started a business that was doing well enough to afford her twenty-thousand-dollar fee. The second half was being held by a bank that would release it when she showed them the photo. She'd learned early not to trust people to follow through with the final payment, or as she liked to think of it, her success bonus. Her very first client had stiffed her once she had her son back, giving a sob story instead.

Rox left through the back of the building to avoid drama in the lobby with the reverend. Her client would do the same. Marty had probably already escorted Jonah from the building. Her stepdad was an ex-cop and could take care of himself, but she called him anyway. "Are you out?"

"Yep. That bastard came at me when he realized the girl wasn't coming back, but I hit a few of his pain centers, and he decided to cooperate. I'll be at the meet-up spot in five minutes."

She walked a few blocks to her car, then drove another three to join Marty, who was already in his own car. They usually took both in case circumstances called for it. He got out, gave her a high five, then burst out laughing. "I dig the adrenaline rush of messing with assholes to rescue someone in need."

"Me too. See you at home."

Marty gave her a mock salute and drove off. She'd loved seeing him in uniform when she was a kid and had followed him into law enforcement as an adult. But the department had stuck her in tech support after a year on the street. She'd been disappointed but not surprised. The way her brain worked, with its atypical neurologics, made her a great data cruncher. But after six years spent cyber hunting addicts and thieves, she'd gotten bored and joined the CIA. Hoping for fieldwork, she'd ended up as an analyst again. After her sister, Jolene, died, Rox had left the agency and started an investigation firm. Now she was her own operative and doing pretty well. With any luck, the treatments she was about to start—a new form of magnetic brain therapy—would make her even better.

Successful missions were essential. She'd failed to rescue Jolene when her sister was in a cult-like multiple marriage. Rox had taken an overseas CIA assignment instead, and Jo had been murdered by the cult leader while she was gone. Rox would never forgive herself. But she was doing her best to make up for it.

Twenty minutes later, she parked at the bank as her work cell phone rang. Assuming it was her current client, she picked up. "Is everything all right?"

"No. Is this Karina Jones?" The woman's voice was tentative and stressed.

Jones was the code name she used with clients. Another one already! "Yes. Who is this?"

"My name is Jenny Carson. My husband, Dave, and I need your help."

"Who referred you to me?"

"Detective Scott Monroe."

Rox didn't know Monroe personally, but she knew of him. She and Marty had put out the word about her services among select law enforcement people with the understanding they would pass it along to others they could trust. Only her first circle of close friends knew she conducted extractions. Beyond that, clients knew her fake name and paid in cash deposits, including some that went directly into a bank account.

"What kind of help do you need?"

"Our daughter joined that charity cult, Sister Love, and we haven't seen her in months. We're worried sick." The woman choked back a sob.

Another extraction so soon? Rox didn't feel ready. And she was supposed to start her therapy tomorrow. But the woman sounded so desperate. Plus, the group mentioned was local, so she wouldn't have to travel. "What specifically are you worried about?" A rescue target had to be at risk for her to take the case.

"We think the leader is keeping her captive. Other girls work in their soup kitchen, but Emma doesn't, and we haven't seen her since she joined." The mother burst into tears.

This grief she understood. "Have you been to the police?" *Of course they had.*

"They won't help us. Emma is eighteen, and she joined Sister Love willingly." Jenny Carson had to stop and take a deep breath. "After we didn't see her at the soup kitchen, we asked the police to check on her. But even if they knew where the cult members lived, they can't go in there without a search warrant, and they say we don't have a real reason to think anything is wrong."

Rox understood the legal limitations officers faced. "Do you have any evidence that your daughter is being abused or restrained?"

A telling pause. This time, Dave Carson spoke, and she realized they were on speaker phone. "No, but they prey on vulnerable girls. We think the leader trolls online for conversations about suicide."

A flash of rage burned in Rox's chest. This was a new low. "That's deplorable. Do you know his name?"

"Yes." Mr. Carson was still doing the talking. "We called the state office where charities have to register, and it was founded by Deacon Blackstone and Margo Preston."

Deacon? She hoped that was his name and not his religious title. The other person, Margo, might not even exist. "How did he contact your daughter?"

"Online." Mrs. Carson was still fighting for control of her emotions. "Our girl was in a car accident, and her best friend died." Another sob. "Emma was devastated, and she joined the group out of guilt. I'm afraid he'll ruin her life."

Rox knew she would take their case. "Okay, I'll meet with you, but I have conditions. Such as, you can never tell anyone where my office is or discuss the details of my services—unless you're sending me someone who needs my help. Did Detective Monroe mention my fee?"

"He said you were expensive, but money is no object."

Good to know. "I'll need ten thousand in cash up front. Bring it with you when we meet. If the case has unexpected expenses, we'll discuss them at the time. If I'm successful, I get another ten grand. Are you fine with that?" Rox sometimes reduced her fee for clients who couldn't afford her rate, so she had to get full payment from those who could.

"Of course. We just want our daughter back."

"Come to my office tomorrow morning at ten. Bring photos of your daughter, a large one and a wallet size. I'll text you directions and instructions later today." At the moment, she was still in Salem, fifty miles south, and had to pick up her payment from the bank, drive back home to Portland, and wrap up the details of her current case.

It was unusual to have another extraction so quickly. She often went months without a call and had to supplement her income with routine investigative work. But she itched to get started. After seven years as a cop and ten with the CIA, she loved the thrill of the chase, even when it was all on paper. Plus Deacon Blackstone seemed like a dirtbag predator, and she couldn't wait to extract Emma from his clutches.

CHAPTER 2

Rox glanced at the clock. *Yikes!* She'd been dancing for forty minutes and was running late now. It was easy to get caught up in the music, the moves, and how dancing made her body and soul feel. God, she loved it. Except for hiking—which took her to interesting wilderness places—she hated all other exercise.

She quickly showered and dressed for her appointment in nice pants and a button-up blouse. Blue, of course, the only color she wore. She chose a serious-but-friendly cobalt blue, saving the lighter shades for dates and other nonwork activities. She liked blue because it muted her reddish skin tone and looked good with her dark hair and eyes. Sticking with one color made shopping and dressing easy. Her current boyfriend had bought her a pale-pink blouse to try, and she really liked him, so she'd put it on. But wearing the odd color had made her so uncomfortable, she'd asked him to take her home to change. How long would he put up with her quirks? He'd made it six months, so far.

As Rox blow-dried her short hair, her phone rang, and she almost didn't hear it. *Kyle!* She'd missed two of his calls while working out. Rox pulled on her wireless receiver, a habit from her days at the agency, and answered. "Hey, Kyle. Sorry I missed your calls. I'm getting ready to meet with a client, then I've got my first TMS treatment."

"I know. I just wanted to say good luck." He sounded both excited and worried. "Please tell me you're not doing this just for me. It has to be what you want."

She wanted normalcy. To feel the emotions of the music as well as the beat. To be able to wear pink and not feel self-conscious. To finally look into people's eyes and know what they were thinking.

"Rox?"

"I want this treatment. I'd been mulling it over even before I met you." Yet her relationship with him was now a driving factor.

"Okay. But know I love the way you are."

Love? He'd never said that before. Nervousness overcame her, and she laughed. *Of all times!*

"See? I like that you think it's funny."

Now she was confused. "I have to get going. Thanks for calling. I'll see you later." She hung up, wishing she'd said something affectionate back. But he hadn't actually said he loved her. He'd said he loved "the way" she was. Very different. She started to text him but heard a familiar knock.

Rox pulled on black sneakers, hurried to the living room, and called, "Clear!" A cop's term for *safe* or *okay to enter*.

Her stepdad hurried in.

"Hey, Marty. What's up? I'm running late."

"Let me go with you to your doctor's appointment. There's no reason to do this alone."

Except that she wanted to. "I appreciate your support, but it's not necessary. Besides, you'll be bored, sitting in the waiting room while I get the treatment."

"I'll be bored *and* worried sitting here." Much shorter than her, with cropped silver-blond hair and blue eyes, Marty was her physical opposite.

By *here*, he meant the other half of the duplex they shared, with him as the owner. She'd moved in after leaving the CIA, thinking her stay would be temporary until she found her own place. But she liked the quiet southeast neighborhood, and the rent she paid was far less than its market value. Back then, Marty had still been working, so she hadn't seen much of him. That all changed when he retired and she started her PI business—and his proximity was both a blessing and a curse. "It's transcranial magnetic stimulation," she reminded him. "Not heart surgery. It'll be easy and painless."

He pushed past her and stood in the middle of her living room. "You really should let me paint a few walls. All this beige is depressing." She ignored his home-improvement suggestion, and he got back to the subject at hand. "We both know it's not about the treatment, but the aftermath. You could be overwhelmed."

That was her fear as well, but also the reason she had to go alone. What if she freaked out and started crying for the first time in her adult life? She couldn't bear to let Marty see it. "They say the effect could take a few days to fully kick in."

"And it could be immediate. I've been reading up."

The magnetic pulse stimulated nerve cells in the brain. It was more commonly used to treat depression, but it was also sometimes effective in helping people on the autism spectrum deepen their emotional intelligence as well as think and function in a more neuro-typical way. Part of her hoped for a miracle, and part of her expected to be disappointed.

"I'll be fine. Time to get going." She hurried toward her bedroom and called over her shoulder, "I'll tell you about a possible new case when I get back."

Marty followed and talked nonstop while she put on makeup. When he moved on from the treatment to the need to replace her countertop, she tuned him out. One of the small blessings of being neuro-atypical.

◆ ◆ ◆

Thirty minutes later, Rox walked into the small office she rented under her Karina Jones name. In the year and a half she'd been a private investigator, she'd done four extractions and broken only minor laws, but she never wanted to face a kidnapping charge, which carried a minimum sentence of seven and a half years in Oregon. It was even longer in other states, such as Utah, where she'd traveled to take an assignment.

She passed through the foyer—which held only two comfortable chairs and a desk with a monitor—and entered the next room, her office. Rox locked the door behind her, grateful for the second exit that led into a narrow alley behind the building. She hoped to never have to use the back door to avoid a client or law enforcement, but she had to be ready. She turned on the communication system at her adjustable desk, which she kept at standing height. She wouldn't be here long enough to worry about getting comfortable. Online research could be conducted at home, and everything else was fieldwork. All she did here was meet with clients, including for some routine PI cases such as missing people and tracking cheating spouses.

The Carsons weren't due to arrive for another ten minutes, but she heard a car pull up. *Good.* She hated when people were late, especially herself. She turned to the monitor, where she watched the outer door open and the couple enter. Rox leaned toward the speaker. "Hello. This is Karina. Have a seat, and we'll get started."

The woman, a heavyset bleached blonde, looked confused, but her husband—taller, leaner, and gray—quickly sat down. Dressed in a suit, he looked like the businessman he was.

"Where are you? Why aren't we meeting in person?" Jenny Carson stood behind the other chair, biting her lip. Her pretty face pulled attention away from her ample hips, and her black cashmere sweater was fashionably long.

"Because I have to protect myself." Rox worried that Mrs. Carson might not be able to handle the arrangement, but Rox couldn't compromise on her protocols. On their monitor, they could see her at the desk, but her face was pixilated to obscure her identity. She tried to reassure the couple. "I'll do everything I can to extract your daughter legally, but my fee is twenty thousand because I'm prepared to take her physically and bring her to you. That's also known as kidnapping. If it goes down that way, you won't be able to identify me or testify against me." She knew the Carsons had the money because she'd checked them out. They lived in Lake Oswego, and Dave Carson was an investment banker.

Mrs. Carson finally sat down. "I understand."

"Did you bring cash?"

Dave lifted a satchel to the table. "Yes. Do you want to see it?"

"No, that's fine. Tell me what you know about the Sister Love charity."

"Not much. They're very secretive," Dave said. "Other than the soup kitchen address, the website doesn't have contact information, except for an email link. The state office for charities doesn't have a residential location for them either. So we don't even know where Emma is."

Rox googled the charity's name and landed on a bare-bones website. "You said Deacon Blackstone was the founder?"

"Yes," they said together.

"Give me a minute." Rox accessed a federal database—with a password supplied by a friend inside the agency—and found a brief file. Normally she did some research right away, but after yesterday's extraction and drive home, she'd eaten a late meal and crashed, so she was just getting to it. Scanning the text, she learned Blackstone was an army veteran with a handful of medals. But a year after his discharge, he'd spent four months in jail for assaulting a girlfriend, then disappeared off the radar. No address or employer was listed. Rox felt a flash of fear for the Carsons' daughter and a shiver of worry for herself. The cult leader was a potentially violent opponent with military training.

"Can you even find her?" Jenny grimaced and bit her lip.

"Most likely." Almost everyone was traceable. If some of the young women were coming out of the cult residence to work in a soup kitchen, Rox might be able to simply follow them home in the evening.

Dave cleared his throat. "Even if you can't get her out, at the very least we need to know she's alive. We're worried that Emma might have left the cult and become a victim of the I-5 Killer."

Oh god. In the previous six months, three young women—all blonde, thin, and estranged from their families—had been found dead along the interstate corridor between Salem and Portland. "Did you bring the pictures? Hold up the big one for me, then leave them both on the desk."

With shaking hands, Jenny held up an eight-by-ten color photo.

Emma Carson had long white-blonde hair and a narrow pretty-doll face. *Damn.* Rox hoped she'd never have to tell these people their daughter was dead. She tried to reassure them. "The odds of her being a serial-killer victim are very slim. But I should be able to determine if she's still with Sister Love. Even if she's not, I'll help you find her."

"Thank you."

"What else do you know about them? For example, where is the soup kitchen?"

Dave gave the address, a location on the edge of Portland's Chinatown and not far from a huge riverfront park. "We've been to the Sister Love mission a few times to ask about Emma, and they say she's fine. But we don't believe them. And they won't talk about the founders. When we tried to press the girls for answers, they called the police."

"I can try a different approach." She may not have been a field agent, but she'd worked with enough to know their tricks. "Tell me about Emma, about her personality. I particularly need to know what she likes. I may be able to draw her out with an appealing offer."

"But how? There's no way to contact her!" Jenny held back tears.

Rox tried to will the other woman to keep herself together. "I'll find a way. Just tell me everything."

"She loves horses," the father offered. "But she gave up riding after the accident."

"She gave up everything!" Jenny blurted. "She was so distraught. She talked about suicide all the time."

At least the Sister Love charity had kept her alive. Maybe. "What else does she like besides horses?"

"She loves music, especially Adele and Taylor Swift." Mrs. Carson glanced at her husband. "Emma's also an artist. She draws the most beautiful fantasy images."

"Maybe I can work with that. Did she ever talk about attending art school?"

Jenny Carson seemed to know more about her daughter than her husband did. "She was enrolled at Portland State, but never went to classes after the accident."

"What did she take with her when she left home?"

"Not much," Jenny said. "The charity makes the girls turn over all their belongings, so she doesn't even have her cell phone anymore."

That sounded more like a cult, and a sting-type extraction might be tough with Emma. She'd been raised with money, so luring her out with a financial reward probably wouldn't work this time. Especially if she wanted to punish herself by living without luxuries. Plus, the girl was emotionally unstable with suicidal tendencies. Maybe the only option was to go in gangster style and just take her. Either way, Emma would need serious counseling to keep her from going back. "Have you thought about deprogramming? I mean, if I get her out?"

Dave stiffened. "Yes, of course. We'll get an expert lined up."

"Okay. I'll come up with an idea for reaching her. But I won't share it with you. The less you know, the better." Rox wanted to protect them from potential prosecution as well. Also, she didn't actually have a plan yet, just an idea. She would brainstorm with Marty, and maybe call her friend in the agency. They would find this girl. And bring her home. "I need you to deposit the second ten thousand in the Pacific Crest Bank."

Rox rattled off the account number. "The bank will only release the cash to me when I bring them a photo of you reunited with Emma. If I don't produce the photo within a year, they'll return the money to you."

Jenny scowled again. "Why is all that necessary?"

"It guarantees my payment."

They still looked confused.

"That way you don't forget to pay me after you have your daughter back."

"Oh, I see." Mr. Carson nodded. "So this is our only in-person meeting?"

"Yes. Unless I need operating expenses beyond what I expect, or unless I need one of Emma's personal items to use as part of a ruse."

More confusion from the Carsons. Rox added, "That's not likely. Leave the cash, and do not talk about our arrangement with anyone. I'll be in touch." She clicked off the camera feed, worried she would be late for her treatment.

She'd left her office with forty minutes to spare, but being nervous and distracted, she still missed a few turns and had to backtrack. In Portland rush hour traffic, that could be a nightmare, but this morning she lucked out and there were only minor incidents. She arrived at the neurology clinic fifteen minutes early and checked in with a medical assistant.

"The first appointment canceled, so they're ready for you now. I'll take you back." The assistant stood, and her head came only to Rox's shoulder. She looked up at Rox and smiled, then started down the hall. Rox followed, her stomach clenching for the first time.

"Everything still the same?" the assistant asked. "No new implants?"

Rox shook her head.

"Any new medication?"

"No."

They entered a room at the back of the building.

"Have a seat in the chair, and the doctor will be right with you."

Rox paced the room instead. This would be the easiest medical appointment she'd ever had. No need to get undressed. No strange, cold hands probing private parts. No uncomfortable discussions. Yet, it might change her life . . . though maybe for only a while.

The chair was really a padded lounger, like in a dentist's office. Except instead of an overhead light at the end of an arm extension, this setup featured a metal coil that would attach to her head. Did she really want to mess with her brain chemistry?

Yes. Being able to read people's expressions and emotions would make her more effective at her job. A lot of her private investigative work was small-time stuff that required her to gain information from people. Subtlety and deception were often necessary. Those skills would make her better at the big extractions too. Her neuro-atypical quirks had made her superiors think she was unsuitable for fieldwork at the CIA, and she was eager to prove she could be an effective operative. Her unusual brain, which loved numbers and patterns, made her an excellent analyst, but that wasn't enough.

The door opened, and she turned to face the doctor, an older woman with a loose gray bun and purple-framed glasses. They'd met at a previous appointment to evaluate her for the treatments. "Hello, Rox."

"Hello, Dr. Benton."

"Do you have any more questions before we begin?"

She'd already asked a dozen. "No."

"Then have a seat and get comfortable."

Rox eased into the chair. This would be the first of a ten or so treatments—depending on how she handled them—and she had to let go of her anxiety.

The doctor handed her a pair of soft earplugs. "First, I'll have to determine the right dose of magnetic energy. I'll pulse you with greater doses until your fingers twitch. Then I'll set the level, and we'll begin the treatment, which should take about forty minutes. You'll hear clicking sounds as I do the pulse."

Dr. Benton pulled the extension arm next to Rox's head and gently placed the attached coil on her forehead. "Ready?"

Rox laughed. "Yes, but is the world ready for the new me?"

An hour later, she was driving home, feeling exactly the same, except for a soreness on her forehead where the magnet had pulsed. She decided to have lunch with Marty to discuss her new case, then stop by the Sister Love soup kitchen to scope it out. Emma's situation challenged her, and Rox was eager to get rolling. She exited the expressway and stopped at a traffic light, noting the roadwork ahead. Time for a little music. Rox grabbed her phone and clicked on a favorite song, "Higher Love" by Steve Winwood. Except for all of Queen's songs, it was about the only music she listened to that didn't have a heavy dance beat. After a moment, the melody engulfed her, its haunting beauty filling her heart with sadness and longing. She was so overcome, she pulled over and shut off the song. Warm tears began to roll down her face.

Oh god, what had she done?

CHAPTER 3

By the time Rox arrived at home, she felt fine. Her response to the music must have been a fluke. A one-time reaction to the new neural connections she was making. Her brain would adapt. She stepped out of her Nissan Cube, bought to accommodate her height, and rain pelted her as she ran for the house. Spring in Oregon—seventy and sunny one minute, fifty and wet the next. By the time she'd finished a quick blow-dry of her hair and blouse, Marty was back with his familiar knock.

"Clear," Rox yelled as she headed up the hallway. She met him in the kitchen. "Lunch?"

"Sure. What are we making?" Smiley and lighthearted, her stepdad was an odd matchup with her. As he had been with her mother. But Marty had been the one who raised her and Jolene on his own after Georgia had left them.

"Let's keep it simple," Rox decided. "I need to start working the new case this afternoon."

"PB&Js it is."

Rox laughed. Marty could eat peanut butter sandwiches every day of his life. She'd had her fill long ago, but she wouldn't argue with him. Often she had lunch by herself at the food cart outside the Woodstock branch of the county library, where she volunteered a few hours a week. They loved her speedy cataloging ability, and she loved the smell and feel of books, even though she did most of her reading digitally now.

Watching Marty spread peanut butter as though he were creating art put her in a good mood, so she poured two glasses of milk and added dark-chocolate syrup—a favorite from her childhood meals with him. They sat down at the small round table in the breakfast nook, rain beating on the nearby window.

"Okay, I waited." Marty looked at her expectedly. "What was it like? How do you feel?"

As she finished a bite of sandwich, Rox thought about how to describe the treatment. "A little weird, but painless. I could feel and hear the magnetic pulses, but it's not something I can articulate." She tried anyway. "Sort of like a gentle pressure."

"How do you feel now? Any different?"

"I'm good. Happy." She didn't plan to tell him about her first time crying over a sappy song.

Something in his eyes shifted, and she realized he was disappointed. "What's wrong? Don't you want me to be happy?"

Now he looked startled. "Of course I do. Nothing is wrong. I was just hoping you would notice a difference."

"I have." She put down her sandwich, suddenly not hungry. "I just saw in your face that you were disappointed, and it made me feel bad. I'd never experienced your disappointment before." She had disappointed her mother plenty, but Georgia had always said it out loud.

"You must be reading facial cues better." He grinned. "I'll have to be more careful around you."

"Really?" Marty had always seemed so obvious and easy to read.

"I'm joking, for Pete's sake. I hope the magnets don't ruin your sense of humor." He downed a slug of chocolate milk.

"Not with you around."

They laughed, then finished their sandwiches.

"Now tell me about your new client."

"Dave and Jenny Carson. They want me to get their daughter back from the Sister Love charity, which may be a cult."

"Never heard of it."

Rox summarized what little she knew and added, "I plan to stop by their soup kitchen this afternoon and get a sense of how many young women work there and how many are on the residential property, wherever it is."

"What can I do?"

"Help me brainstorm a ruse. Emma is motivated by guilt, and I think the way to bring her out is to offer her another way to atone."

"Like another cult?"

"Or another mission, such as an opportunity to travel somewhere and feed the poor in another city."

"But you would have to offer it to the other girls too, or it might be suspicious."

He had a point. "Any other ideas?"

"The inheritance thing worked well."

"Not this time. The Carsons have a lot of money, so Emma won't be motivated by it."

"But the cult leader will." Marty cocked his head to the side. "Where do they get their funding?"

"Good question." Rox thought about other cults and how they operated. "They usually make the members turn over whatever cash and belongings they have. Some groups, like the Moonies, send their followers out to beg in the streets."

Marty was silent, and she knew he was thinking about Jolene, because she was too. They'd both lost their favorite person the day Imam Sadat had shot all nine of his wives, then turned the gun on himself. Egomaniacal types were unpredictable. Another reason to move quickly.

"Did I mention that Emma hasn't been seen in a few months? I wonder if Blackstone is keeping some members close to home for . . . proprietary reasons." Rox meant sexual abuse, but she wouldn't remind her stepdad that Jolene had likely been a sex slave. If only they'd known more and acted earlier . . .

"He could be the type." Marty's expression was tight—angry and sad at the same time.

They both had to deal with this issue every time they took an extraction case. But Marty had taken Jolene's death harder than she had. Jolene had been his baby, his only biological child.

"I'm fine," he snapped, as if reading her thoughts.

"Me too." Rox stood, unsure. Would her new brain patterns make her unsuited to the work? "I'm going to the soup kitchen. I might dress as a homeless person."

Marty jumped up. "Or a nun. That way you could get information and see how the members react to being recruited to another group."

Brilliant. She walked over and kissed his forehead. "Great idea. Thanks."

He looked up at her with an unexpected joy.

Had she never expressed that kind of affection before? "We'll save the homeless-guy gig for you, in case we need to go back." She winked. "You're more suited to it anyway."

On the drive downtown, she stopped at a Party! Party! Store that carried a few costumes year-round and rented a black nun's habit. After she paid with some of her clients' cash, she asked, "Do you have a restroom I can use? I need to put this on now."

The young clerk laughed. "Normally we don't let customers use our employee bathroom, but this I want to see."

Was he mocking her? "You should see what I had on yesterday." She smiled and threw the heavy costume over her shoulder.

The man laughed, then led her into a small back office, where he opened a narrow door. "Here you go." The facility was about the size of an airplane bathroom, and she didn't know if she had enough room to change. At nearly six-foot and 170 pounds, she needed more space than most women. But this time of year, it was too warm to put the habit on over her clothes. She nodded at the clerk, stepped in, and made quick work of it, only slamming one elbow against a wall when she pulled on the detached headpiece.

The young clerk had gone back to the front counter, and she waved at him as she hurried out of the shop. A couple passing on the street raised their eyebrows. Rox smiled. Even though it made her nervous, she loved fieldwork. Too bad the agency had kept her at a desk all those years.

The soup kitchen sat on a small triangle block in an old building that had once been a restaurant. Despite its proximity to the river and downtown businesses, this area on the edge of Chinatown was a mecca for the homeless. A cluster of ragged men loitered in front of the decrepit storefront. Rox entered the property from a side street, parked behind the building, and glanced up. "Keep Portland Weird"—the city's motto—was painted in giant letters on the back brick wall. Rox smiled. She did her part. In fact, her own peculiarities made her accepting of other people. Yet her need for order and predictability often clashed with the chaos Portland sometimes offered. The naked bike ride, for example, that hundreds participated in every year was totally unsettling, but with plenty of pre-event warning from news sources, she could avoid seeing it.

She dug out her wallet and checked Emma's photo again in case the girl was inside. Glad for a break in the rain, she climbed from her car and walked slowly around the building and inside, rehearsing what she would say. She wished she'd taken more time, maybe printed up some fake promotional material.

The facility was larger than it looked from the outside, with twelve or so tables and seating for about fifty people. At this point in the afternoon, they were between meals, and only a handful of people were hanging out—a woman with two small children and three men, all over fifty. Or they looked that old. Being outside all day, every day, aged people's faces, and it was often hard to tell. The mixed aromas of baking bread and week-old sweat confused her senses.

A long cafeteria-style counter separated the dining area from the kitchen, and Rox spotted a girl pulling large metal trays out of the serving area. Two more young women were at the back of the kitchen washing dishes. The woman at the counter looked up, her long ash-blonde hair pulled back in a ponytail. "How can I help you?"

"I'm Sister Helen," Rox blurted. *Stupid.* Hopefully this girl didn't know about the famous nun from that *Dead Man Walking* film. Rox reached out a hand. "And you are?"

"Bethany." A deep sadness was etched into her otherwise plump young face.

"Nice to meet you, Bethany. I admire the work you do here. I'm sure it pleases God as well."

"Sister Love's mission is to serve others, but we're not religious."

Had she blown it with the nun getup? "You don't have to be religious to do the right thing. Your heart is obviously in the right place."

"I'm trying." Bethany gestured at a tray of baked rolls. "Are you hungry?"

"No, but I'd like a cup of coffee if you have one. And I'd like you to join me for a moment."

The girl's haunted eyes widened. "Why?"

"I want to know more about Sister Love. I'm from St. Paul's Church, and we'd like to support what you do here. It aligns with our mission to serve the needy."

"Uh. Okay." The girl moved to a tall silver coffee urn, filled two foam cups, and came around the counter.

Rox tried not to look disgusted by the meltable white container. She didn't have to actually drink the coffee. They sat down at a table in front. "How old are you, Bethany?"

"Nineteen."

"How long have you been a part of Sister Love?"

"About a year. Why?"

"Just getting to know you." Rox noticed the girl's dark-hazel irises. "Your eyes are beautiful. I've never seen a color like that before."

Bethany smiled shyly. "They change. If I wear green, they look green. If I wear dark colors, they look kind of caramel." At the moment, the girl wore blue nurse scrubs. *Odd.* Rox glanced at the kitchen and noticed the other girls were dressed in scrubs too. A uniform that stripped the members of their individuality. "You're lucky. I'm stuck with boring brown eyes."

Rox picked up her coffee, realized it was too hot to sip, and put it back down. "Tell me about this organization. For starters, who runs it? And how are you funded?"

"You ask a lot of questions."

Rox smiled, hoping she looked unbothered by the comment. "As I said, our church would like to support your mission, but we have to make sure your goals and methods are aligned with ours."

"We have a simple mission to feed homeless veterans, and I think most of the funding comes from donations." Bethany lowered her voice. "Some of the members go out in the evening to ask travelers for money."

That sounded hinky. Rox wanted to press for more information, but she had to be careful and get the basics before the girl walked away. "So if our church decided to make a large donation, who would we contact?"

Bethany hesitated. "Our leader likes to stay in the background, but I'm sure he'd want to take your offer. You can email him. Deacon at Sister Love dot com."

It was a start. "Do you have a personal email address, Bethany? I'd like to correspond with you."

She blinked. "Why?"

"Because our church needs committed, caring people like you. I want to send you some information about our mission."

"Thanks, but I'm content to stay with Sister Love. It gives my life meaning." A wave of sadness washed over her face. "If that's even possible."

Another kitchen worker walked over to the table. A chubby woman, she looked older than Bethany, maybe twenty-five, and had the thick skin and toothless jawline of someone who'd been homeless. Rox realized none of the girls were likely minors. The cult leader was careful about age of consent. Did he have sex with the members?

"Hey, Beth, we have work to do." The other woman's swollen hands were on her hips.

"I know. Save some for me. I'll be up in a minute." Bethany gave the older member a nervous glance, then turned back.

Rox reached over and patted her hand but kept quiet until the other woman walked away. "Don't get in trouble on my behalf."

"It's fine. Ronnie worries too much."

"About what?"

Bethany shrugged. "Everything. We all have baggage."

"I can help you unload some of your troubles." *She was so off script.* "I can help all of you. How many people are in the group?" She didn't dare ask about Emma directly.

Bethany downed her coffee and stood. "I can't tell you that, and we don't need your help."

Rox had to take a final shot. "If you know someone in your group who wants to make a bigger commitment and sacrifice, send her to me." Rox started to write her burner-phone number on a napkin, but the young woman scooted away without comment.

"Thanks for chatting with me." Rox stood too, walked to a trash can, and tossed her coffee. With a sideways glance at the back of the kitchen, she noted the third young woman's face. Not Emma. Too bad she hadn't learned anything about her clients' daughter. But she would be back. Outside and out of sight, she jotted down the members' descriptions and what little she had gathered about the group. She'd wanted to take photos, but it would have been too blatant and weird.

Before leaving, she scanned the sign on the front door. The charity served dinner until eight. After cleaning up, the crew would likely leave sometime between eight thirty and nine. Perfect. Dark enough to follow them without being spotted. If she found their home base in time, she might be able to follow the members who went out at night. She didn't buy the *soliciting-donations* line. What the hell were they really up to?

CHAPTER 4

Later at home, Rox got online and learned that Sister Love had been operating for nearly three years. The Portland newspaper had done a story about it, but Deacon Blackstone had given only a single comment about his commitment to helping homeless veterans. *How had the reporter reached him?* The article mentioned the Sister Love soup kitchen had originally served only veterans, but they'd found it too difficult to screen and turn away the non-vets who showed up. But ex-military clients were given preferential treatment. The news piece also suggested the charity had cult-like traits, claiming the volunteers all lived together and had turned over their possessions to the founder. But there was no mention of recruitment tactics. Rox wondered where the Carsons had found their information about the charity's online trolling. Maybe they'd assumed it from their daughter's experience.

Another extensive search for Blackstone himself revealed almost nothing. No social media presence and nothing newsworthy. But his exclusive young-female membership made her distrust him. He had a dark secret somewhere; she just had to find it.

Maybe a bitter ex-member. If she could locate one. Sister Love hadn't been operating long enough for anyone to age out yet, but it seemed likely that someone had left the group in the last three years. She would rent the nun costume again tomorrow and pay the soup kitchen another visit. Tonight, she would follow the members when they left and stake out their home base. Working late called for another cup of coffee.

Rox brewed a small pot, noticed the blue sky out the kitchen window, and took her coffee out to the back deck to make a few phone calls. The first was to a close friend at the CIA. While the phone rang, she wondered what she would do for background intel if Sergio ever left the agency.

He came on the line. "Hey, Rox. Give me ten seconds to send this email." She counted while she waited.

"Sorry," he said a few moments later. "I'm buried in paperwork."

"Seventeen seconds. You're losing your touch."

He laughed, but it wasn't his usual bellow.

"Is everything all right?"

"Mostly." A moment of silence. "Sherry was diagnosed with breast cancer."

What a terrible thing. A sadness overcame Rox. "I'm so sorry."

"They caught it early, and it's treatable, so let's not talk about it."

That was a relief on both.

"I can't believe you even noticed something was wrong," Sergio said.

It was unusual for her.

Before she could tell him about the magnetic treatments, Sergio asked, "How's the PI business?"

"Good. I completed an extraction yesterday and got a call for another assignment on the drive home."

"You must have really gotten the word out about your services."

"Marty's and my contacts in the police department helped a lot. He's a pretty good wingman too." Rox decided to get to the point before she ran out of small talk. "The new extraction involves a charity called Sister Love, run by a man named Deacon Blackstone. He's an army veteran, and I'm hoping you can call your contact at the Pentagon and get me some background."

"Sure." He paused. "Ex-military men are usually weaponized. Promise me you'll be careful."

"Always. Physical confrontation is a last resort."

"Good. What else do you know about Blackstone?"

"Not much. The Sister Love website doesn't even mention his name or background. And no one seems to know where he and the members live."

"I'll make the call now and see what I can find."

"Thank you. I'd love to find something I can use as leverage."

"I'll be in touch."

"See ya." Rox hung up. The combination of hot coffee and late-afternoon sun had overheated her, so she went back inside to her desk. She checked her notes, then called the newspaper and asked for Jordan Ackers, the byline on the story she'd read earlier. A young-sounding woman answered. "This is Jordan."

Should she give her real name? Not to a reporter. "This is Karina Jones, a private investigator. You wrote an article about Sister Love last year. I'm trying to reach Deacon Blackstone, and I'm hoping you can give me his phone number."

"I don't have it. I emailed him through their website, and he finally responded with a one-line comment."

"Any idea of his location?"

"Nope. And believe me, I tried. The members must be sworn to secrecy, because they wouldn't tell me anything about the founder or where they lived."

"Did they give any hints? Such as mentioning a dorm or a house?"

"One of the girls used the word *farm*, so I suspect they're in a rural setting."

It was something. "How many girls did you talk to?"

"Just two at the soup kitchen. They both swore that all the members are eighteen or older."

"So Blackstone is careful to avoid custody issues or statutory rape charges."

"If he's porking them, but they won't talk about that either." The reporter made a slurping sound, as if she was drinking through a straw. "What's your interest in Blackstone?"

"I have a client who's trying to find him."

"Call me if you do. I'd like to write a follow-up story." She hung up.

Was Blackstone paranoid or just incredibly private? Paranoid types made her nervous. They tended to perceive everything as a threat and respond accordingly. Rox looked at her phone. *Damn.* She was running late again. She sometimes put on a dress for her dates with Kyle, but not tonight. She might need to drive straight from the restaurant to the soup kitchen so she could be there when it closed. She texted Kyle, aka, Detective Wilson: *I'll meet you there. I have to work later.* She would miss their post-dinner sex, but this assignment felt urgent. The more she learned about Blackstone, the more dangerous he seemed.

Kyle sent back an emoji frown. He would miss the sex too. Rox rolled deodorant under her arms, brushed her teeth, and headed for the door. Her phone rang with the sound of a bugle playing reveille, her ringtone for Marty. She took the call, knowing he would try again until she got back to him. "Hey, I'm headed out to meet Kyle for dinner."

"I won't keep you. I just want to know if you have an update on our case."

He wasn't officially her partner. The PI business was registered in her name only, and she employed him for special circumstances. But she discussed every case with him—because it was helpful to her and gave him something to focus on. "Not much. I visited the soup kitchen this afternoon, and I've got a friend at the CIA digging into Blackstone's military career." Rox stepped outside, locked the door, and walked to her car.

"You're wearing pants. Are you working after your date?"

The old snoop was watching her from his front window—and was still sharp enough to connect the dots. "Yes, I'm going back to the soup kitchen."

"Tailing one of the members?"

"Yes."

"Let me keep you company. I'll meet you there."

She'd known he would say that. "It's not necessary for both of us to probably waste our time. And if we chat, we could miss something."

"Okay. Call me if you need help."

"Always." He'd taken it well. Rox waved at his front window as she backed out of the driveway. Marty was annoying, but he was the only father she'd ever known, and she loved him fiercely. He'd married her mother, Georgia, when Rox was six, and she'd bonded to him in a way that surprised everyone, including herself. Two years later, her baby sister had been born, and Georgia had named her Jolene, in keeping with the family tradition of naming females after hit songs. When Rox was thirteen, her mother had landed a role on Broadway—an opportunity of a lifetime she'd called it—and moved to New York for what was supposed to be a few months. She'd never come back, except to visit. Marty had raised her and Jolene by himself and had always treated her like his own child. She called him Marty, not Dad, because her mother had always insisted on being called Georgia. So it made sense to her brain. The terms *mom* and *dad* could be vague and confusing. Everyone had parents of some kind, and she preferred specificity.

When Rox arrived at Sweet Basil, Kyle was already seated at their favorite table—near the front, but against the side wall. He'd been a beat cop for ten years and a homicide detective for six. But she'd been a cop *and* a CIA agent, so she liked to keep her eye on the door too. Because he still carried a weapon, she deferred and let him have the lookout spot. As she approached, the sight of his broad, handsome face made her heart swell. Rox walked to his chair and kissed him, then sat down, surprising herself.

Kyle's forehead wrinkled. "Hey, I thought we didn't do public displays of affection." He was forty-two but had gray at his temples and sun-weathered skin from a lifetime of hiking.

"Sorry. I'm just happy to see you."

His eyes widened. "You had your first treatment today. How did it go?"

"The process was what I expected, but becoming emotional on the way home while listening to music was quite a surprise."

"Just from the music, huh?" An amused smile.

Maybe she shouldn't have told him. He wanted her to be more flexible and privately affectionate, but not a sentimental fool. "It was weird. But I'm sure it was the newness of those neurological connections. A one-time quirk."

"Yeah, that makes sense."

A server approached the table. He nodded at Rox. "The usual? Crispy basil with chicken and a pot of jasmine tea?"

Should she look at the menu for once? Not tonight. She didn't have a lot of time. "Yes, thank you."

Kyle asked about the specials, then ordered a beef-and-mushroom dish. After the server walked away, Kyle asked, "What else is different?"

She wasn't sure she wanted to tell him but felt compelled to. "I'm more in tune with people's emotions. Even listening to my friend laugh over the phone, I could tell something was wrong."

"That's a good thing. And I noticed you hesitated when he asked if you wanted the usual."

Rox laughed. "I know. I thought about looking at the menu. I hope I don't become one of those people who can't ever make up their mind."

He laughed, smiling widely. "You won't."

"I know. I'll still be me."

"I hope this makes you happy."

"Me too."

The waiter brought their drinks and started to set them down on the wrong sides of the table. All three of them laughed.

When he stepped away, Kyle said, "Tell me about your new case."

Relieved to be on a neutral subject, Rox summarized what she'd learned but didn't name the group or her clients. Keeping those secret protected Kyle from knowing details that might hurt both of them—especially if she had to resort to illegal methods.

Their food arrived, and while they ate, Kyle talked about the stress of working the I-5 Killer case. She suggested they take a vacation together when it was over, and they joked about all the places they would never go. Neither of them did well in crowds.

After dinner, he walked to her car and whispered in her ear, "Come over when you're done working if it's not too late."

"I was hoping you'd say that." She stepped back, resisting the impulse to kiss him again. "I'll text you."

Rox climbed into her vehicle and watched him walk to his. Would they still be compatible if she kept doing the treatments? She hoped so. Kyle was a great guy who could be very tender in intimate moments, and he seemed to like her quirks. And now that she was forty, finding a new boyfriend could be challenging. Her attraction to law-enforcement types already narrowed the field.

Twenty minutes later, she parked a block away from the Sister Love mission. A few scruffy men sat on the sidewalk in front of the soup kitchen, one with an oversize backpack and another clutching an overstuffed plastic bag. They seemed to be engaged in an animated conversation. A pretty sunset bathed the street in a pink glow that softened the dingy setting.

Rox climbed out of her Cube and crossed the street to check out the back parking lot of the soup kitchen. Her hope was that the Sister Love members had arrived—and would leave—in one vehicle. If they didn't, she would follow Bethany, the girl she'd chatted with earlier. The more Rox knew about her, the easier it would be to gain her trust and maybe turn her into an asset. Rox assumed the girls all lived together because that was typical of cults. The leader always wanted control. But what if they were scattered across several houses or locations? Finding Emma could be challenging. She hadn't given the Carsons a timeline, and she hoped they were prepared for the long game.

The back lot was exposed on two sides, and the only cover was a big maple tree in the corner. Rox stood behind it and checked out the vehicles. A long white passenger van, like churches always used, sat near the back door, while two small cars and an old truck took up the area closest to the nearby laundry. The van likely belonged to the charity. Its lack of logo was in keeping with Sister Love's low profile.

Rox hurried back to her vehicle and reparked near the corner where she could see the soup kitchen's back door, plus the side of the building where the van would likely exit. But the triangle lot offered several exit possibilities, and she couldn't watch all sides. Tension built up in her chest, and she had to force herself to relax. This could be a long wait.

But the schedule ran as she'd predicted. At 8:32, five women came out the back door. The older one, Ronnie, headed for a separate car, and four other girls climbed into the van. Rox hadn't seen the fourth one earlier, but maybe she'd come in just for the dinner shift. She was short and chunky and took the driver's seat. Definitely not Emma. The van backed up, and Rox noticed Ronnie's car was already gone. The older member obviously had privileges the others didn't. Maybe she didn't even live with the group. Rox's instinct told her to follow the van. The younger members were likely headed back to the main residence.

The white van pulled out, and Rox fought the urge to start her car immediately. After a count of five, she eased onto the nearly empty street. *Damn!* Where was some traffic when you needed it? But the young women probably weren't watching for a tail. Or maybe they were. If their leader was paranoid enough to stay off the grid, he might have trained his followers to be leery. Rox hung back and tried not to worry. But the sun had set, and noticing another car's headlights in the dark was the easiest way to spot a tail.

The van took Route 26 to the 205 and headed south. Once they were on the highway, Rox closed the gap, leaving only one large SUV between them. Ten minutes later, the Sister Love van took Highway 212, an exit Rox wasn't familiar with. She'd grown up in southeast Portland and worked a central-city beat as a police officer, then moved to Washington, DC, with the CIA. Now she lived in the same general area where she'd grown up, only a little nicer. She'd explored some of Portland's suburbs, but this was Clackamas County, and she didn't know it well. She kept her eye on the van, figuring she could correlate road names on a map later.

They passed a McDonald's on the right, where a group of young people stood around sports cars in the parking lot. Moments later, a mobile-home community appeared on the same side of the road. *Riverbend.* Oh right. The Clackamas River was out there somewhere in the dark. Not many trailer parks had a view of the river. Abruptly a big-assed Cadillac pulled out in front of her. The old man driving didn't even look her way. Rox hit the brakes and cursed. Now she had a slow-moving vehicle between her and the SUV—and the van in front of it. Passing the old man could draw attention. *Too bad.* Rox waited for a minivan going the other way to pass by, then pressed the accelerator and flew around the Cadillac.

Up ahead, she saw only one pair of headlights. Was that the SUV or the van? She kept her foot on the gas and closed the distance. It was the gray car. Where the hell were the members? The SUV's turn signal came on, followed by brake lights, and it turned down a street lined with new homes. Rox stared down the exit road as she slowly passed. No second car lights, just the SUV. Had the van turned off somewhere while the Cadillac held her back? She hadn't seen another exit. Gunning the engine, Rox raced forward. The van must have simply pulled ahead.

A split in the road gave her pause, but Rox spotted lights in the distance and kept to the left. *Please let it be the van.* Rox pushed her speed a little higher. The roar of an engine startled her, and she glanced in her rearview mirror. Two sets of headlights barreled up the road behind her. For a moment, she feared they were after her. But the lead car blew by her, with the second one only a few yards behind. The sports cars she'd seen at the McDonald's—and they were racing!

The two vehicles screamed down the highway and quickly disappeared into the darkness, without veering to pass a van. Where the hell had it disappeared to now? Rox saw a side road and slowed. She glanced down the lane but didn't see any headlights. Unsure, she drove forward. Another side road appeared. She braked and turned down the lane. No cars were on the road. She drove slowly, passing an occasional house, but didn't see any white vans. Some of the homes were set back from the road, with adjacent barns and surrounding fields. Other homes were newer, with smaller lots. Eventually the road dead-ended, and she turned around, feeling conspicuous. The van could have parked behind a farmhouse, and the cult members could be inside, watching her drive back and forth.

Damn. She'd really messed this up. No, she'd done everything right. Sometimes, shit just happened. She drove back to the first side road, turned off her lights, and crawled along. This road was more rural, with fewer houses, set farther back. Some weren't even visible, just a mailbox and driveway to indicate their presence. The darkness was frustrating, but at least she had some moonlight. After a mile, she turned around and drove back. When she reached the main highway, Rox pulled off to the side. She hated to give up and go home, but it made more sense to come back tomorrow in the early light of day before the members went out again. She started to pull out, but the sound of racing engines caught her attention. Rox paused and waited for the sports cars to scream by her again. Crazy kids. She hoped no one got hurt. A different engine rumbled in the distance behind her. Rox glanced in the rearview mirror. Headlights pulled out of a driveway and turned in her direction. By the height of the beams, she knew it was a large vehicle. The van?

Rox slumped down in the seat. It was too late to move her car farther off the road, but at least her lights were still off. A minute later, the big white van pulled up to the intersection, only ten feet away. She glanced over and noticed that the young woman in the front passenger seat was a different girl from any she'd seen leaving the soup kitchen. She looked younger, with long hair. But that was all she could tell in the dark. Was the driver different too? In her quick glance, she thought she'd seen four or five people. Had the van stopped somewhere and swapped out members? What the hell was going on?

CHAPTER 5

Rox waited a full minute before easing onto the road. The van had turned the way it had come, toward the Portland suburbs. Not surprising. The other direction led to more farmland, wilderness, and a small town named Boring. But where were the Sister Love members headed at nine o'clock in the evening? To solicit donations like Bethany had mentioned? But where?

On the drive back, the darkness and lack of traffic gave her nothing to focus on, so Rox played math games in her head. For fun, she tried to predict how long it would take to arrive at their likely destination somewhere downtown, based on speed and her best guess about distance. Twenty-seven minutes. Rox checked her watch so she could test her answer later.

She wished she knew how many members were under the influence of Sister Love. Four had worked at the soup kitchen, and maybe five members were in the van now, most likely a different crew. Based on everything she'd learned about cults, she tried to calculate the exact number of young women in Sister Love. At any point, Oregon was home to seven to ten of what could be called cults, if you didn't count nudist colonies or national groups like the Moonies. She also excluded the Rajneeshees, a group of two thousand that had occupied an area not far from here thirty years earlier. Small localized cults usually had ten or twelve members, but maxed out at about forty. All-female cults were usually more harmonious than mixed-gender groups, so they operated for longer periods of time. Considering the uniformity of the members' ages, her best guess was thirteen or fourteen, with very few having left the group—which reminded her that she needed to try to find an ex-member to interview.

As they approached the 205 freeway, a few more cars entered the road, and Rox eased in closer. She expected the van to get on the express-way, but which direction? North would take them back toward the soup kitchen and all the suburbs east of Portland. To her surprise, the Sister Love members headed south, which quickly turned east toward the I-5 freeway. At the split, the van continued south, surprising her again.

Twelve minutes later, it exited onto a side road leading to a huge truck stop, complete with fueling station, small convenience store, and restaurant. *What the hell?* Rox passed the driveway—in case they were watching—then turned around and parked across the street at another gas station. She glanced at her watch. Twenty-five minutes. Two min-utes off her estimate. Not bad, especially since they'd driven in a com-pletely different direction from what she'd predicted. Rox reached under her seat for binoculars, then positioned herself as low as she could in the car and still have visibility.

Four young women climbed from the van, all wearing dresses or skirts. Three had long hair, and all were slender and attractive. *Interesting.* Bethany, the girl she'd talked to at the soup kitchen, had long hair but was heavier and rather plain. And Ronnie, the older one, had been downright unattractive. Rox had to conclude that this was a specialized mission that required the girls to be pretty. She pulled out Emma's photo again and studied it. She didn't think her x-target was in this group, but Rox couldn't be sure until she saw them all closer up. She watched them cross the parking lot toward the café, two of them carrying small round objects. Donation cans? The girls kept glancing down the long row of semitrailer trucks in a side lot and talking quietly. The truck stop was probably loaded with guys, many at the end of their driving day. The whole scenario gave Rox a bad feeling.

An older man with a bushy gray beard held open the café door, grinning as the members entered. Rox ditched the binoculars and climbed from her car. She had to find a better vantage point, one where she could see what was happening inside. She hoped this wasn't about prostitution, but the possibility was pretty strong. She crossed the road, glancing around for something to duck behind. *Oh, never mind.* She would just go inside. The restaurant was huge, and she could stay near the front. Or hang out in the little next-door store.

As she strode through the front parking area, counting nine regular cars, a shiver ran up her spine, startling her. That had never happened before. Rox spun around, but there was no one behind her and no one inside any of the cars. Yet she sensed someone watching. She glanced at the side lot where the big rigs were parked, angled in next to each other like giant dominoes. Two men stood near a truck in the middle, talking, but they weren't looking at her. The tall light poles were thirty yards apart and illuminated only small areas, so if someone was watching, he could be hiding between trucks.

Rox shook it off and hurried into the little store, immediately spotting the double glass doors that opened into the diner.

"Hi." The thirty-something guy behind the counter barely looked at her, keeping his focus on the tiny TV near the register.

Rox walked to the magazine rack near the door and picked up a copy of *Newsweek*, the only readable publication in a cluster of covers with nearly nude women. After flipping it open, she continued her surveillance. Through the glass doors, she saw the four cult members head for a booth near the back. Two of the girls sat down, while the other two began to circulate the room, carrying gold canisters. They stopped at tables where families or couples were seated—highway traffic, the people from the cars in the front lot. Rox couldn't hear what the members said, but after a short pitch, most of the diners put money in the offered cans. It seemed like an odd place to solicit donations, especially this late.

The other two girls accepted coffee from a waitress who stopped at their booth, but neither picked up a menu. After a few minutes, a tall man in a knit cap got up from a bar stool at the long counter and walked over to the girls' booth. Dressed in jeans and a windbreaker, he looked about forty-five. He spoke directly to the girl who'd been driving, then walked out of the restaurant. Rox would have paid a hefty bribe to hear that conversation. Another minute passed. The two girls with the donation cans kept working the room while the two in the booth sipped their coffee. Abruptly the girl he'd spoken to—with long dark hair and tattooed arms—got up and sashayed toward the front door. She glanced in Rox's direction, so Rox turned away and looked down at her magazine.

Her phone vibrated in her jacket pocket, startling her. She had it on silent, and except for clients, she didn't get many calls. She reached in to quiet the phone, then glanced through the glass doors again. Tattoo Girl wasn't in sight. Rox shoved the magazine into the rack and turned to the front of the store. The girl had to be outside. Rox started for the door, and her phone buzzed in her pocket again. Someone really wanted to talk to her. What if it was Marty? Sometimes his bad knee locked up, and he couldn't move. She'd gotten good at massaging the stubborn tissue until it was ready to cooperate. Rox slipped the phone out and looked at the caller ID. Yep, it was her stepdad. She stopped near the front door, keeping to the side, and took the call.

"I'm still tailing the cult members," she whispered. "Can this wait?"

"I'm on the floor, or I wouldn't have called."

"Are you hurt?"

"Not much, but my knee is locked up, and I can't move."

"Call 911."

"It's not that serious; I'll wait until you get back." The old man hung up.

He was so damn stubborn. But she didn't blame him. The thought of being picked up and hauled off by paramedics made her shudder too. Rox stepped outside, looking around for the tall trucker and/or the tattooed member. Neither was in the parking lot. They had to be inside one of the trucks, most likely exchanging sex for money, which would make Deacon Blackstone a pimp too. Rage and disgust burned in Rox's gut. She wanted to snap kick the bastard in his face. The force of her reaction made her laugh out loud, a strange, harsh sound. If everyone could feel anger this acutely, no wonder the world was so violent.

She wanted to intercede in Tattoo Girl's activity but couldn't risk revealing her face up close—or her mission. Rescuing Emma was her priority, and she still had no idea where the girl was. But after she returned Emma to her parents, she would go after Blackstone with every police contact she had. She hoped like hell Emma hadn't been working as a prostitute. The Carsons would be devastated.

Rox started for her car. The only other thing she could accomplish here tonight would be to follow the girls home and find the exact location of their base. But even that was iffy. The rural highway wouldn't have any traffic this late, and her tail might be too obvious. And right now, Marty needed her.

Inside her car, she picked up the binoculars, scanning the side parking area for one last look. Near the middle, she spotted Tattoo Girl in the passenger seat of a big rig. She was looking down as if reading a text message. The truck driver was slumped against the driver's side door, mouth moving and eyes flickering.

Was he drunk? Or maybe drugged?

Damn. She needed to get going, but this was too strange to turn her back on. She decided to watch for another minute or so. Headlights coming off the freeway made her slump low in her seat. Rox waited for the car to pull in across the street and shut off its engine before she eased back up. With her binoculars, she found the occupied truck again. The driver was still slumped over, apparently sleeping, and the cult girl seemed to be looking for something in the cab. His wallet? Was this a roofie-and-roll operation? Considering their supposed mission, that seemed especially sleazy.

Loud voices boomed in the parking lot across the street. Rox turned her binoculars to the three people who were climbing out of an SUV that had just parked. Young men who sounded drunk. Another car caught her eye. Someone occupied the driver's side, sitting low like she was. She couldn't determine the gender. The person wore dark clothes with a hood. An undercover officer? Did the police know about the members' activity here, whatever it was?

Rox's phone vibrated again, and she took the call. "Has anything changed?"

"I'm dragging myself to the toilet, but I don't how I'll get up there to use it."

"Hang on. If I push my speed to seventy, I'll be there in—" Rox did a quick calculation. "Eighteen minutes." She started the car and drove off, glancing in the rearview mirror for one last look. The watcher was still there.

CHAPTER 6

Wednesday, April 19, 6:35 p.m.

Deacon Blackstone opened his phony "Angela" Facebook page and did a search for the word *suicide*. After finding only a single non-useful instance among his connections, he quickly moved to Instagram. The girls on this site were often too young to recruit, but it was his best source so far. He'd found Skeeter at an AA meeting, but that had just been luck, and she hadn't panned out for family cash or sexual willingness. But she was a hard worker who worshiped him, so no regrets. But at the moment, Instagram was a bust, so he scanned several western-state news sites for car and shooting accidents involving young girls. He'd found Bethany that way and still couldn't believe his good fortune. The trifecta of guilt, family money, and sexual willingness was rare, but after Bethany had come Emma. Margo had found her, and there was definite promise there. But he'd learned not to count on anything, so he was always on the lookout for fresh *golden girls*.

The *Seattle Times* reported an accident involving a seventeen-year-old named Megan Grimes. The driver of the other car, a father of four, was in a coma, and doctors didn't know if he would live. A surge of excitement rushed through him. This lead had potential. Her age bothered him only because of his healthy fear of statutory rape charges, but she could turn eighteen next month, so he tried to find her online. Megan had a Facebook page, but not many friends. Better yet. She also hadn't posted in two weeks, which wasn't encouraging, but he sent her a friend request anyway. Recruiting her might take months to accomplish, but probably not much time on a daily or weekly basis. Once he'd sounded Megan out, "Angela" would mention the Sister Love charity and see how she reacted.

Deacon glanced at the clock. It was time to go. He shut off his computer, grabbed a jacket, and headed into the wide hall. He hoped not to run into any of the residents, including his girlfriend, Margo, on his way out. He had dealt with all the female bullshit he could handle for the day. He made it outside with only one brief encounter. The sun was setting as he climbed into his Bronco, but Deacon didn't mind driving in the dark. Margo worked the graveyard shift at the hospital, and they were both late-night people. Plus he liked having the road to himself.

Forty minutes later, he pulled into the Linnwood Care Facility and headed inside. The girl at the reception counter gave him a friendly greeting as he passed. He'd visited many times already, and they all knew him. The young ones liked him, but the older gals were pretty cold. *Fuck 'em.*

He knocked on the door of his father's room, waited a few seconds, then stepped in. The old man's hearing was shot, so he often didn't even respond. Tonight he looked up from his reading and smiled. "Deacon. What are you doing here?"

Visiting, like he did most Wednesday nights. Deacon walked over and patted his dad's shoulder. "Thought I'd drop in and play some checkers." The old man liked the game, and it gave them something to do together. Regular conversation had become impossible. His dad looked shriveled too, as though his body were drying out like an apple left in the sun. Christ, it was hard to see him this way. Yet it was perversely satisfying too.

"You're on."

Deacon got the board from the closet and set up the pieces. After the first game, his dad took a break to watch one of his shows. Deacon let his mind drift between making responsive grunts to his father's comments. Afterward they played another game, but halfway through, his father lost his focus and started mumbling about one of the caregivers.

"What a dumbfuck move," the old man said suddenly, staring at the board.

"I think that's the game." Deacon glanced at the clock. It was after nine, and visiting hours were over. That bitch of a nurse would barge in any moment and remind him. Deacon got up from the small table and walked around to the back of his father's wheelchair. "I've gotta go. You need anything?"

"Get me the hell out of here."

"Besides that." No way in hell could he take care of the old man. Even though his girlfriend was a CNA, she refused to consider it. His dad needed too much hands-on wiping and feeding. And he got mean again sometimes. He'd been abusive to the whole family when Deacon was a kid—only back then, he hadn't realized other dads weren't like that. Then the old man had mellowed a little after Mom died. Now that his mind was going, he was reverting back to his true self. But here in the private nursing home, they had orderlies and medications to deal with him. Deacon patted his dad's shoulder. "I'll see you next week."

"Bring Tess."

Who the hell was Tess? Deacon had learned not to ask. "I'll try." He grabbed his jacket and stepped toward the door, hoping to get out before Nurse Ratched came in.

The door opened, and a big, ugly woman in pink scrubs stood there with a tiny woman in a gray suit. *Too late.*

"Mr. Blackstone, will you come to the office? We need to talk." The little one motioned at him to follow.

Deacon kept moving, and they stepped aside to let him leave the room. At six-three and 240, he found that not many people stood their ground in front of him. He turned left, ignoring their request.

They followed him, still yapping. "You need to get caught up on your payments or find another facility." The tiny woman's voice was both shrill and loud, like a mean little dog.

Deacon choked back a response that would have made his army buddies blush. "You'll get your damn money." He glanced back and made eye contact just long enough to shut the bitch up, then strode down the hall to the side exit.

Seven grand a month was fucking outrageous, and the old man's pension covered only part of it. Deacon had exhausted his own personal savings after the first six months. But paying the old man's bill gave him a source of pride, as if he'd finally done something his dad could respect. Now he was behind on two payments and didn't know how long he could hold them off.

A couple of the charity's new recruits had family money, and he was working on a plan to unload some of it, but these things took time. Emma was especially skittish about discussing her parents, but he was making progress. She was warming up to him physically too. Keeping her at home in the complex was crucial to his seduction strategy, but she was a virgin—and still withdrawn from her accident—so it could take months to win her complete confidence. He needed another fast-track plan to round up some cash.

Out in the parking lot, he gulped in fresh air. The damn nursing home always smelled like shit. For that much money per resident, you'd think they could afford some disinfectant. Deacon climbed in his Bronco and stared at his cell phone. *Just call him!* He had a friend, an old army buddy, who owed him a favor. They hadn't talked in a while, but Deacon had kept tabs on Greg and knew he was doing well financially as a realtor. They would call it a loan, with the unspoken understanding that it might never be paid back. *Oh fuck!* He hated to ask a friend for money. Only for his father . . .

Deacon looked through his contacts, relieved to find the number still there. He changed phones every once in a while and always bought prepaid anonymous devices with cash. He kept his name off everything. By now his name should have just about disappeared from public records. Except his military service, of course, and he regretted that whole bullshit experience. The government had no business in his personal life or finances, and now with the internet connecting everything, it was more important than ever to stay under the radar.

He couldn't call Greg without downing a beer first. He drove down the road to a tavern, noticing a rehab center across the street. The reformers and do-gooders were everywhere. But they attracted insecure and guilty girls and could be a good source for recruits. But not tonight. He didn't have the focus for it. Deacon went inside, ordered a house tap beer, and stared at the bartender's boobs while he pounded it down. She was too fleshy and jaded for his taste. He liked lean, young, and pliable.

After sitting just long enough to let the alcohol hit his system, Deacon headed for the parking lot without leaving a tip. Not after paying five bucks for a beer. In the car, he pulled out his phone, and it rang in his hand. *Margo.* He wasn't in the mood to deal with her. "What's up? I'm just leaving the nursing home."

"Nothing. I just got to work and wanted to say hi before my shift started."

She wanted him to feel guilty for not saying anything to her before he took off. "Yeah, we kind of missed bumping into each other today." Margo was unpredictable, a mix of sweet nurturer and harsh taskmaster. She'd been his caregiver for a week after a motorcycle accident. One day, she'd given him a blow job as he lay there helpless, and he'd become infatuated. She'd shared his antisocial attitude, and they moved in together a month later. He'd lost interest in her after a few years, but she made a good partner for the charity, and she gave great head. Unlike the younger girls, who either didn't like sucking cock or didn't know what the hell they were doing.

"How's your dad?" she asked.

"The same." He stepped out of the Bronco and lit a cigarette, only his third of the day. "The little Nazi who runs the place ambushed me on the way out and demanded I get caught up on the payments or find another home for him."

"It's a bluff. They won't kick him out."

Margo sounded confident, as always, but Deacon knew better. "Yeah, they will. They'll dump him at an urgent care place or a hospital. We need some cash. And right fucking now. Any likely donors?" While he looked for new recruits, Margo trolled for bleeding heart suckers on social media sites. She had a couple of phony GoFundMe sites going too. The soup kitchen cost real money to run, and they never had enough. But he liked feeding veterans, maybe the only worthwhile thing he'd ever done.

"No, but I'll make some calls tomorrow." He heard an odd sound in the background. Then Margo said, "Maybe we should hit up Emma's parents for a donation."

"We will, but I still think it's too soon." He took a long drag of nicotine.

"Deacon." She paused. "When we score that big pile of cash from her, let's be smart. Shut down the charity, take the money, and get out of town. Go someplace warm and dry."

This again. Fuck, she was annoying. "Not while my dad is living his last days." Even after the old man passed, he would probably find another excuse. He liked controlling and screwing the girls. The thought of a life with just Margo freaked him out. So boring. So . . . unsatisfying.

"He might live for years," she complained.

"I hope he does." He felt obligated to say it, just to put her in her place, but he was tired of this conversation. He still loved his dad, but the man he visited had become a stranger. And the monthly payments were crushing him.

"See you in the morning." Margo hung up.

Deacon was glad he hadn't mentioned his plan to call Greg for money. If things went badly, Margo would never know he'd tried and failed. He climbed back in his rig, found the number again, and pressed Call. His fists clenched while it rang. Maybe Greg had a new number. He finally picked up and said hello.

"It's Deacon."

"Hey, buddy. How the hell are you?"

The familiar voice brought back that good feeling of knowing someone had your back. The only good thing about serving in the military. "I'm all right. And you?" Deacon started the Bronco and frowned. The engine sounded rough. He'd have to check it out tomorrow.

"Can't complain. Although I do anyway." A booming laugh followed.

Deacon realized how much he missed Greg, one of the only men he'd ever bonded with. As much as he loved women, being surrounded by them 24/7 could be draining. "You still play b-ball every damn day?"

"I'm down to three days a week." A pause. "What are you up to? Last time we talked you were looking for work."

Deacon hesitated. No one knew where he was or what he did. Could he trust Greg? Probably. "I never found a job, so I created my own. I run a soup kitchen for homeless veterans." That was one version of how it happened. He'd really wanted to do something noble for other veterans, hoping to impress his father, who thought his service in Afghanistan was a waste of time—unlike the old man's service in the "good" war, World War II. Margo had gone along with the charity, but on the condition that they kept some of the money they would collect for themselves. Then her estranged daughter, Ronnie, had showed up again, and Deacon had sent her out to panhandle for donations. That had got him thinking about young girls with low self-esteem and how easy they were to manipulate. The Sister Love idea had blossomed from there. A way to help his war buddies, earn some respect and money, and surround himself with pretty young things at the same time.

"Dude, that is some serious shit," Greg responded. "Good for you."

Deacon laughed, trying to keep it light. "The charity keeps me out of trouble."

"Do you operate on donations?"

"Mostly. We also have a small grant from a larger foundation." More bullshit. They'd been turned down repeatedly, but the lie made them sound legit.

A pause. "Is that what this call is about? Are you looking for a donation?"

"Sort of." Deacon's stomach clenched. "My dad's sick, slowly dying, and his nursing home is costing me everything." It was now or never. "I was hoping you would loan me some money. Just short term."

"How much?" Greg's tone was wary.

"Twenty grand, if you can spare it." Suddenly nervous, Deacon put the car in gear, eager to be on the road.

"Holy shit. I don't have that kind of money."

Liar! "Can you get it for me though? I wouldn't ask if this weren't important."

"I'm sorry about your father, but I need cash too. We're trying to have a baby, and we need in-vitro treatments. Even with insurance, our twenty percent will be at least ten thousand, and Kerry will need time off work too."

Just what the world needed, another fucked-up kid. "Come on. A baby can wait a little while. My dad is dying." Deacon took a left out of the parking lot and headed for the highway.

"You can't just call me after four years of silence and hit me up for twenty large. It's bullshit!"

Four years had gone by? Deacon felt his face flush. The bastard had conveniently forgotten his promise. "Hey, you owe me. I saved you from being court-martialed. And you said I could call in a return favor. Anytime!"

Greg made a scoffing sound. "So you lied for me. I know it was a risk, but it didn't cost you any time or money."

Rage gripped him, and Deacon had to pull off the road. "Don't make it sound like nothing. We both could have been locked up. I saved your ass, and now I need your fucking help."

"You prick!" Greg's voice blasted in his ear. "You sold military fuel to Afghans and pocketed thousands of stolen dollars. If I turn you in, you'll go to prison."

Oh crap. He couldn't believe Greg was using that against him. "Everyone did it, and you wouldn't rat on me."

"Yeah, I would. Because you also sexually harassed my wife. Yes, Kerry and I are married now, and she would love to get even with you."

"Oh, come on. That was a decade ago and stupid guy stuff. My dad is dying, and I know you have the money to help me."

"Here's another idea," Greg shot back. "Find a rich donor for your charity, then funnel twenty grand to me, so I can give Kerry a baby. You owe her, you prick."

What the hell was he talking about? Some fertility crap? "Fat fucking chance." Deacon started to hang up.

"I'll report you!" Greg shouted. "If you don't send the money in the next two weeks, I'll turn you in for theft. The army may not prosecute you, but they will strip you of your medals."

The fucker! The Distinguished Service Cross and the Silver Star were the only decent things he had to show for his life. "You won't do that."

"Yes, I will. It would make Kerry quite happy. She would rather have the in vitro treatments and the baby, but seeing you dishonored would be almost as good." Greg let out a harsh laugh. "Thought you would blackmail me, huh? Not your best idea, Deacon. Get the money, you son of a bitch." Greg hung up.

What the hell had just happened? Shaking, Deacon put his phone back in his pocket and pulled onto the road again. Would Greg really report him for selling fucking gas to the locals? He had to be bluffing. *Fuck!* What a disaster. Now he needed more money than ever. And Emma's parents had it. Time to turn up the heat and get between that girl's legs. Once he'd fucked her and the oxytocin was flowing, she would bond to him and give him whatever he wanted.

CHAPTER 7

Thursday, April 20, 8:05 a.m.

Emma put down the last pan of muffins and joined the other girls at the cafeteria table. Only seven people this morning. Who was missing? Deacon hadn't joined them, but he often didn't. Or sometimes he came late. Oh, Bethany wasn't there, but she might have just slept in. The sisters ate in shifts, with soup kitchen workers and house helpers like herself eating first, and the donation takers eating an hour or so later. Emma cooked and served both meals, then cleaned the kitchen, alongside either Jewel or Skeeter.

They joined hands and said their own version of a serenity prayer, ending with, "I give my life in service so that I may find peace."

After a quiet moment, Emma asked, "Where's Bethany?" She leaned forward to catch Ronnie's attention.

"How should I know?" Ronnie shrugged and kept eating. She was twenty-three, but looked forty. Most of her back teeth were missing from meth use, and her face was pockmarked. She'd been with Sister Love since it started and was the only member who had her own car and didn't have to wear scrubs all the time. Emma tried not to be jealous.

"Bethany's still sleeping." Skeeter barely looked up from her eggs when she spoke.

"Oh right. It's her day off from the soup kitchen." Ronnie gulped coffee and made a face. "What is this crap? What happened to the good stuff?"

"I don't know." Emma knew it wasn't her fault. "Margo does the shopping. I just brew it."

"Just be grateful we have coffee," Skeeter chimed in. "None of us deserve the good life."

For once, Ronnie had nothing to say. The conversation at the other end of the table went quiet too, and Emma lost her appetite. She would never forgive herself for the accident. She rubbed her thigh, the tenderness still with her. The cut to her leg from windshield glass had not been life threatening, but she wished it had been. Thoughts of suicide had controlled her life for months, but only her mother's watchful eye and the guilt of hurting her parents had kept Emma from following through with her death wish.

Then Deacon had found her online and offered her a chance to atone—and a new life that would help her undo some of the damage she'd done. Emma had moments when she hated the confinement of Sister Love and moments when she hated herself. But most of the time, she felt peace—content to take care of the house and the other sisters, who understood and shared her guilt and were giving their time to homeless people. Someday she would go out and serve at the soup kitchen or collect donations, but for now, Deacon wanted her home, where he could counsel her and keep her safe from self-harm.

Just as she thought about him, she heard his voice and looked up.

"You're not eating." His handsome face looked concerned.

Emma's mood lifted. "I'm having a Guilt Episode."

"Food deprivation is not how we punish ourselves." Their leader sat down and helped himself to eggs. "I'll have a special guilt reliever for you after you finish your work this morning. So come to my office."

What did he have in mind? Emma shivered with both anticipation and dread. "Thank you." She picked up her fork and forced herself to eat.

Skeeter, a quiet girl with a freckled face, reached for more eggs, her arm crossing the edge of Deacon's plate. He grabbed the wooden spoon from the bowl and smacked Skeeter's forearm.

"I'm sorry," she said quickly. "I should have said *excuse me.*"

Emma wondered if Skeeter had been impolite intentionally, just to be noticed. Or to be punished. Some members wanted to feel physical pain. Emma accepted it when Deacon meted it out, but she preferred other types of atonement.

They all held their breath in case there was more punishment coming.

"You're excused," he finally said. Deacon picked up his fork and gestured for all of them to do the same.

They ate in silence for a moment. Then Ronnie said, "Let's get going. We need to stock the van with greenhouse goods."

The soup kitchen girls stood and cleared their plates. Emma got up too, grabbing an empty serving bowl with her free hand. While Ronnie and her crew loaded garden vegetables from the panty, Emma and Skeeter cleaned the table. Deacon hugged them both before leaving the room. His embrace felt wonderful, but left Emma conflicted. She didn't deserve his love. As she walked to the kitchen, the darkness of shame overwhelmed her, and the accident replayed in her mind—in full-color slow motion, as usual.

The text from Jason. Looking down to read it, then laughing at his goofiness. Hearing Marlee yell, "Hey!" Glancing up to check the road. Panic, when she realized she was driving off the asphalt. Jerking the wheel back to the left, then spinning out of control. Sickness in her stomach as the car flew off the road and the rock cliff came out of nowhere. Explosive pain in her head as she snapped forward, then back. Sheer horror as she saw the mangled, bloody mess that used to be her best friend. Screaming and screaming until she blacked out, partly from hyperventilation and partly from blood loss.

"Are you okay?" Skeeter stopped washing dishes and put an arm around her.

"Yes. Just reliving a bad moment."

"We all do. You have to let it go. Being here and serving others is how we make it better."

Emma gave her a small smile. "Thanks. Is your arm okay?"

Skeeter glanced down at the red welt. "Of course. I deserve far worse."

Emma's heart ached for the poor girl. Skeeter had killed her own sister in a driving accident. She would probably punish herself for her whole life. Emma hugged Skeeter. "You can atone for it."

"Yeah, but she'll still be dead."

So would Emma's best friend. She didn't know what to say. Or what would eventually become of them. Would they both grow old here? She shook it off. She couldn't see her future, but worrying about it was selfish and pointless. Thinking about her parents made her heart ache, so she simply didn't do it. "We'd better get to work." Emma started mixing another batch of muffins for the second breakfast.

Two hours later, when all the sisters had eaten, the chrome in the massive kitchen gleamed with polish, and the floor looked clean enough to eat off, Emma checked the work list on the wall to see what else she was assigned that day. Margo created color-coded schedules to simplify the oversight of the house, gardens, and livestock care. Emma had laundry today. Not bad. Thank goodness she rarely had to feed the cows or collect eggs from the hens. She hated the barnyard smells. Before moving here, she'd never interacted with animals. Her parents hadn't even let her have a kitten. She hadn't done many chores in her previous life either.

Footsteps behind her made Emma turn. Margo, a petite woman with a heart-shaped face, had a big voice that always surprised her. "When you run my load of clothes, please use the fabric softener I bought."

"I will." They'd never had softener before. It was too expensive.

"And do them right away." Margo gave Emma a tight smile.

Was something wrong? She decided not to ask. "Sure thing. Right after I see Deacon."

Margo's lips tightened. "No, start the laundry first."

Were the founders fighting? She'd never seen them argue. "Okay."

"Then come to my office for your last iron injection. Tomorrow you give blood again."

Emma nodded. She'd donated blood three times already since joining, and the procedure was creepy, but not painful and didn't take long. But she hated needles, and iron injections beforehand were the worst part. Still, she was happy to do it. Giving her blood to save lives was an easy sacrifice. "I'd better get started on your laundry."

Margo suddenly stepped forward and hugged her. "You're doing well here, Emma. I'm so proud of you." The founder hurried off, her sandals flapping against the tile floor.

A hug and praise! From Margo, her mentor. Emma stood for a moment, basking in unexpected pleasure. But she had no right to feel joy, so she shed the hug like a dirty shirt and hurried to the laundry room at the end of the concrete building. The founders had done their best to soften the building with peach paint and houseplants, but it still had a prison-like feel. The dorms especially.

Ronnie stepped into the wide hall from Deacon's office and said, "Hey, Emma. Would you like to play cards with me this afternoon?"

"If I have time. Deacon said he had a special atonement for me today." Emma had mixed feelings about Ronnie's offer. A game of Spades would be a nice diversion, but Ronnie wasn't the best company. She could be nice, but she was unpredictable, and often jealous. Like right now. Ronnie was scowling because Emma would spend time alone with Deacon.

"Whatever." Ronnie walked off.

Emma hurried to the laundry room, found Margo's basket near the door, and opened one of the industrial-size machines. A load of towels was in the bottom, so she pulled them out and tossed them in the dryer. She started Margo's load, then filled the other two machines with the sisters' clothes. They all wore hospital scrubs in various colors, and everything was community property. Every member surrendered her personal clothes when she joined, except for one outfit, which they were all allowed to wear on special occasions. Ronnie, being older, sometimes ran errands for the founders, so she often wore jeans. Some of the other girls were jealous of her special privileges, but Emma felt sorry for Ronnie. She wasn't very pretty and hadn't found inner peace yet. *Not that her looks mattered,* Emma reminded herself. Sometimes her old life, and judgmental way of thinking, still crept in.

A few minutes later, she knocked on Deacon's office door. "It's Emma."

"Just a moment." She heard shuffling, and then he opened the door.

So handsome! Big blue eyes, smooth skin, and the cutest dimples. He was the only old guy she'd ever thought was attractive, except for maybe Brad Pitt.

"Come in." He stepped back and gestured for her to enter. His office held a desk In one corner, but otherwise it was more like a den, with a sofa, television, and minifridge. She'd spent a lot of time in here during her first few weeks, getting counseling and learning to make peace with her guilt and crime. She'd lost her driver's license, but her parents had hired a good lawyer. And she'd only been given a year of bench probation, which meant she didn't have to check in. Emma knew she owed society more than that, and she was happy to be here doing good work instead of sitting in jail.

"Have a seat. Would you like something to drink?"

A soda! A rare treat. "Yes, please."

She sank into the soft leather couch, and he handed her a can of generic root beer. She opened it eagerly and drank a third in one big gulp.

"You were thirsty."

A moment later she burped, and they both laughed.

Emma remembered why she was here and set the can on the end table. She didn't deserve its sweetness. "What's my special atonement?"

Deacon sat beside her, his leg pressed against her thigh. Emma loved the warmth and pressure of his body. She knew the pleasure was wrong, but she couldn't shut down this feeling the way she could others.

"I'm a little worried about you." His voice was soft, almost caressing.

"Why?"

"Maybe you sacrifice too much." He gently squeezed her leg. "We've talked in counseling about why we don't punish ourselves with lack of food." He paused.

She liked how he always said *we*. He was one of them. He'd harmed others too when he was in the military, and that's why he'd dedicated his life to charity work.

"But we haven't really discussed our bodies' other needs."

Was he talking about sex? Emma's chest tightened, and a shiver of excitement ran through her. She tried not to think about sex—or anything she wasn't entitled to—but her body often betrayed her. "What are you saying?"

"You look a little pale, and you seem tense." His arm slipped around her shoulders, and he pulled her close. "I think you need some physical pleasure."

His body felt so good. Too good. She pulled away. "But how is that serving others? I don't deserve pleasure."

"If we don't stay healthy, physically and mentally, we can't do our best social work." His blue eyes drank her in as though she were a cool glass of lemonade. Deacon leaned in and pressed his lips into hers.

Little fireworks exploded in her chest. Emma kissed him back, unable to stop herself. One of his hands slid under her shirt and cupped her breast. This had to be wrong. Did he do this with other sisters? Bethany had hinted at it, but no one ever talked about it explicitly.

A loud knock on the door made them both pull back. Deacon jumped up and yelled, "Who is it?"

"Margo. This is important."

Deacon let out a harsh breath, stood, and opened the door. "What's going on?"

"Bethany's gone, along with her personal things."

CHAPTER 8

Thursday, April 20, 5:55 a.m.

Rox woke to the sound of beeping. She sat up and glanced at the clock. Not even six yet. Why, oh why, had she taught her stepdad to text? At least with phone calls, he waited until eight, a time by which "all decent people were up." She ignored the message while she took a few minutes to pee, make coffee, and take her vitamins. Then she remembered Marty's locked-knee episode the night before and hurried back to the bedroom to pick up the cell. He'd texted: *I'm coming with you on the recon this morning.*

She couldn't tell him no after making him lie on the floor during her stakeout the night before—and he knew that. Had he always been this manipulative? No, but he'd apparently watched and learned from her dear mother, and now he was making it work for him. She texted back: *Research first, then we'll see.*

After a shower, she sat down at her computer and sipped coffee. She was supposed to be taking walks or dancing every morning for exercise, but she was hit-and-miss. It was easier to skip breakfast, which was usually a bowl of Frosted Mini-Wheats that made her feel guilty anyway. But she just couldn't bring herself to eat an "adult" breakfast like soft-boiled eggs and grapefruit.

She opened Google Maps and scrolled to the approximate location where the van had disappeared and reappeared the night before, then switched to Earth view. After ten minutes of staring at close-ups of each home, she hadn't spotted a white van. But the Google images could have been taken years earlier or when the van wasn't home. She had to focus on likely places where a group of people could live. Large homes with lots of bedrooms or properties with multiple dwellings.

Two possibilities emerged. A newer three-story overbuilt home with a matching smaller guesthouse, and a two-story farmhouse with a run-down mobile home behind it. Rox bet on the farmhouse, which also had several outbuildings on the property, as well as livestock, a hen house, and a big garden. Sister Love was feeding a lot of people, so producing their own food made sense. Rox moved her cursor over the house and clicked. An address popped up, and she memorized it as she read it. But she needed to know for certain who lived there. The post office had that information. So did the local utility company and probably an internet provider. Time for a little *phishing*.

Not keen about lying to a federal agency, she started with the utility company that served the area, a little outfit with the cheesy name of Daybreak. For this to work, she had to pretend to be their client. If Deacon Blackstone wanted to be off the grid, he would likely set up the utilities in his partner's name. Rox called their customer service, cleared her throat, and said, "This is Margo Preston. I wanted to report a power outage this morning."

"What's your service address?" A sweet female voice.

"2835 Barton Road."

"I'm locating your account."

A moment of quiet, with coworkers laughing in the background. If the woman came back and asked Rox to repeat her name, the property address probably didn't match the ID she'd given.

"We don't have any sign of a disruption in service there. What did you say your name was?"

"Never mind. I'm sorry to bother you."

Surprised and disappointed, she went back to scrolling Google Earth over an expanded area. In a moment she spotted an oddity. What the heck was that? Three concrete buildings, laid out with two perpendicular ones behind the main structure. The setup seemed like an old jail—except for the windows on one end of the main building that overlooked a huge greenhouse. The two bunkers in back had only high narrow windows. Was it an abandoned county work camp? It sat at the base of a dead-end lane off Barton Road.

Using the general location and county as references, she googled *Damascus prison camp* and came up with several articles. The top story was embedded in a historical website and mentioned that the work camp had been closed in the eighties for lack of funding, then eventually sold to an anonymous private party. Was the Sister Love group living in an old minimum-security county jail? Tracking down the ownership of the property was important, but it could be time consuming. First, she needed to see if it was occupied. She texted Marty: *Ready? Let's take the truck.* They co-owned an old Chevy, using it mostly for hauling yard supplies and occasional investigative jobs like this one.

Her stepdad walked into her house before she finished pouring coffee in a travel mug. His jeans and blue work shirt were perfect for the excursion.

"Grab a couple of our signs," she said.

"Already in the truck."

He would be the perfect investigative partner if he were a little more detached from her. Maybe a lot more detached.

"What are you smiling about?" Marty looked at her the way a cop would.

"Just thinking about how efficient you are."

"Damn straight." He jerked a thumb toward the door. "Let's get rolling.

◆　◆　◆

They stopped behind a coffee shop–bike store combo five blocks from their duplex. Another thing she loved about Portland: the quirky shops. Rox and Marty each grabbed a magnetic "Builder's Electric" sign they'd borrowed from a friend, hopped out, and slapped them on the truck doors. In a rural area like Damascus, the truck might stand out as non-local. But nobody paid attention to contractors' vehicles. They had legitimate reasons to be everywhere.

Back behind the wheel, Marty asked, "Where are we going?"

"South to Damascus and Barton Road. There's an old work-camp-style prison out there, and I think the cult might have moved in."

"No kidding? Are they renting it from the county?"

"It was sold to a private party decades ago, and I have no idea who owns it. Yet."

"A prison!" Marty snorted. "A fitting setup for a cult."

"They could be squatters, with no one really paying attention. The location is pretty remote."

"Ballsy."

Once they were on the freeway, Rox asked, "Any ideas for conning Blackstone into bringing Emma to us?"

"I've been thinking about it. He's ex-military, and we need to exploit that. Appeal to his patriotism with some kind of award or ceremony?"

"Maybe we can find one of his army buddies." But that might be a waste of time. People who served in a war together often bonded for life. The same was true for cops and field agents who kept each other alive. Rox rejected the idea. "Maybe not. He's pretty reclusive. I think we may just have to stage a coup. But a call I made to the utility company this morning gave me an idea."

"Cut the power to the place?"

Rox laughed. "For an ex-cop, you sure think like a deviant."

He turned to grin at her. "I've chased my share, and it's often a fine line between the two anyway."

"I was thinking we might call in a power outage at the address, and when Blackstone and company are distracted by the utility visit, rush in and grab her." Rox tried to visualize the scene. "Maybe that won't create enough time. We'll have to analyze the access around the place."

"He must leave the property sometimes. We could set up a video camera across the road from the driveway, then check—" Marty cut off his thought. "Never mind. That could take weeks, and we don't have that kind of time."

Rox snapped her fingers. "I could send a check meant for the charity, but made out to him personally. He would have to go to the bank to cash it."

"Nope." Marty shook his head. "He could sign it and have one of the members deposit it in an ATM."

"Of course." Rox racked her brain for reasons a person would have to leave the house. "We can't set the place on fire—it's made of concrete." She laughed. "But we might be able to stimulate a trip to the ER."

Marty turned and raised an eyebrow. "How's that?"

"Still thinking. Maybe send him a gift. Something that gives him food poisoning." They both laughed. "I know, too risky. I'm just brainstorming here."

"We need to question his neighbors." Marty's beat cop experience came in handy.

"Great idea, but we'll need to be subtle. Maybe we can pretend to be looking at property to buy."

"Nice touch."

They talked through another round of ideas and rejected all of them. After a minute of quiet, her stepdad asked, "When is your next magnet treatment?"

"This afternoon."

"Want some company?"

"Thanks, but your time would be better spent at the county court-house tracking down the property owner."

"Will do."

Rox had a pang of guilt for sending the old man to do the grunt work that bored her. He was supposed to be retired, but he helped with the fieldwork for the excitement. Cops often became adrenaline junkies and didn't retire well. "But you don't have to. It's a nice day for golf."

He laughed. "If I ever choose golf over working a case with you, just shoot me and put me out of my misery."

Rox laughed too. "Be careful what you wish for."

Twenty-five minutes later, they approached the lane to the old county work camp. There was no road sign indicating a name or even route number. "Pass the turnoff," Rox instructed. "We can't go down the road in the truck. Too obvious."

"What's your plan?"

The area was densely wooded with patches of clearing for homes and fields. After they turned around, Rox spotted a house down the work camp lane in a clearing a few hundred feet from the main road. No cars were visible in its parking area. "Make the turn, then pull down that first driveway and park. We'll cut through the woods."

"Grab the binoculars from under your seat."

Rox reached down and pulled them out. "What do you keep these for?"

"Getting a closer look." He gave her a smirk, drove down the gravel driveway, and parked next to a cluster of thick fir trees.

In the distance, a dog started barking. "I hope no one is home here." Rox opened the passenger door and climbed out. Marty grabbed a handgun from under the seat on his side and joined her next to the truck.

Rox started to comment, then held back. She owned a Glock, but almost never carried it on her body. The last thing she wanted was to exchange gunfire. But she knew there was nothing she could say that would change Marty's mind, and part of her felt better knowing he was armed.

She zipped up her light jacket. "The work camp is a half mile through these trees." She pointed south, down the side road.

"If I'd known the plan, I could have worn camouflage."

His eyes twinkled, and she realized he was kidding. But was it funny? Her new awareness could be confusing.

Marty started into the woods, and Rox followed, her stomach rumbling. Maybe they would stop for a real breakfast on the way home.

Without a trail, the walk was slow and laborious, but still enjoyable. It beat the hell out of sitting at a desk, scanning digital data for anomalies! Which she had done with most of her time at the agency. As they approached the clearing where the concrete buildings stood, two vehicles came into sight, a slate-blue Bronco and a red minivan, both at least twenty years old.

Yes! She'd been right about her hunch that people were living here.

"No white van," Marty whispered.

"It's probably at the soup kitchen." Rox moved behind a big fir tree at the edge of the woods. Beyond it was an open grass field with a massive garden between the field and the buildings. A six-foot wire fence surrounded the garden, which was only partially planted. She scanned the property with the binoculars, settling on the vehicles. But from the side, she couldn't read the license numbers. "I need a better view of the plates." She kept her voice down and started in the direction of the dead-end lane. After a hundred yards, she turned and focused on the cars. The minivan was closest, and she could barely read the number. Rox stepped forward.

Loud barking made them both jump. A big wolf-like dog charged at them from the woods to the south.

"Shit!" Marty reached for his weapon.

"No." She grabbed his arm. "Let's go."

Rox spun around and took off, her stepdad following. They hauled ass through the dense trees, glancing over their shoulders. The dog was following them but from a distance. "It didn't come from the work camp. It might be wild." Adrenaline made her voice sound tight.

"I'll shoot it if I have to."

Rox was mostly worried about Blackstone discovering he was being spied on. She glanced back again and didn't see the dog. But they kept up their pace until they reached the truck.

Inside she said, "I think I got the license plate of the minivan."

"And we got confirmation that the work camp is occupied."

She held up her hand for a high five, surprising herself. Marty laughed and slapped her palm.

Suddenly the big dog leaped on the hood of the truck, barking and snarling. Rox let out a startled yelp.

"Holy shit!" Marty cranked the engine, put the truck in reverse, and gunned it.

The dog slid off, still barking. Marty turned the truck in a fast, tight spin and entered the road.

Rox looked back, hoping they wouldn't be followed.

CHAPTER 9

A few hours later

Rox walked out of her second magnetic treatment with a massive headache. She'd been warned of that possible side effect, but it worried her anyway. Maybe she wouldn't continue. Changing her brain's connections felt so unnatural, like getting cosmetic surgery or trying to be someone she wasn't. Unsure if she had aspirin at home, she stopped at the store and bought some, grabbing a Reese's peanut butter cup from the rack near the checkout at the last minute. Her addiction to them escalated when she was stressed or in pain. She ate the candy on the way home but didn't listen to music, not wanting a repeat of the crying episode.

At home, she checked her text messages. Nothing from her boyfriend. She called him, but he didn't answer, so she left a message. "Hey, Kyle. I need a small favor. Can you get me the name of a car owner? It's for the case I'm working. I'll buy you dinner if you have time." She gave the license plate number she'd memorized, then with her head still pounding, lay down to sleep for a while.

Kyle's return call an hour later woke her from a weird sleep. She sat up and took the call. "Hey. Thanks for getting back to me."

"Of course. How was your second treatment?"

"It gave me a headache, but I slept and it's better now."

"Did you tell the doctor?"

"No. It's not a big deal." She didn't want to talk about the treatments. "Hey, did you get the license plate?"

"Registered to Margo Preston."

"Thanks. What address is listed?"

He rattled off a street in north Portland.

Probably not relevant. "I think that's an old location. Anything interesting I should know about her?"

"One DUI years ago, and her occupation is listed as a caregiver."

An odd mix. "Thanks. What about my dinner invite?"

"I can't. I have a stakeout tonight. We think we have a lead on the I-5 Killer."

"Great news, but be careful."

"You too. I've gotta go."

"See you." Rox hung up and headed for the kitchen. The headache had eased some, but it was still bothering her. She downed a glass of water and another aspirin, then sat at her computer. Her friend Sergio had sent a short email from his private server with the names of three men who'd served in Blackstone's unit with a promise of more information later. She added the names to her paper file, put the document back in the floor safe, and continued her research. News stories indicated that one of the men, Bruce Anderson, had become a local politician and now lived in Vancouver, just across the river from Portland. Blackstone and Anderson lived close enough to have stayed in touch. Rox searched for his contact information and quickly found his web page. Politicians loved publicity. She called the number and got a slick message. His voice was strong and pleasant, and his photo showed a handsome man in his mid-to-late thirties. Or so he looked. She could never tell, and after insulting a few women, she'd quit guessing.

Rox left what she hoped was an intriguing message of her own: "This is Karina Jones, a private investigator. I'm looking for one of the men you served with. A young girl's life could be at stake. Please call me." She left her burner number, careful as always not to get any extraction-related calls on her personal phone. After she hung up, she wondered if it had been a mistake not to mention Blackstone by name. *No.* If Anderson and Blackstone were best friends, that could have backfired, with Anderson tipping him off. She had to sound out Anderson and play this carefully.

The Skype icon vibrated at the bottom of her computer screen, so she opened it and braced herself for the creepy notification sound. The only person who contacted her this way was her mother, and because she rarely heard from her, she always took the call. Georgia's pretty face came into view, perfectly centered on the screen. "Hi, Roxanne."

Rox nodded. "Hello, Georgia." No one but her mother called her Roxanne. She honored her mother's wishes by calling her Georgia instead of Mom, but the selfish woman had never done the same for her by calling her Rox. "Is everything all right?"

"Yes, I was just cast in a new play I'm excited about." Her mother beamed. She was mostly a voice actor and audiobook narrator now, but she still took acting jobs when she could get them.

"Congratulations! I'm glad you're still getting roles." Rox had made peace with her mother's abandonment long ago and accepted whatever Georgia had to offer. It wasn't much.

"Me too. It gets harder every year, and I'm thinking about a face-lift."

Rox didn't really care. "Be careful about choosing a great cosmetic surgeon."

"Of course. I know just the guy." Georgia leaned forward. "What's new with you?"

"I started a magnetic stimulation treatment for my brain."

Her mother's brow pinched. "For your disorder?"

"We don't call it that, but yes."

Georgia's eyes rolled up, a nervous tic she had. "You're obviously still anal."

It hit Rox like a punch in the gut. The eye rolling wasn't a tic. Her mother had been making fun of her all her life!

"So what are the effects of the treatment?" Georgia asked.

Rox thought of several things to say, none of them pleasant. "For one, I notice now when people roll their eyes and mock me. I have to go." She clicked the icon to close the video call.

She moved away from the computer, her emotions in turmoil. Hurt, anger, and confusion all fought to surface at the same time. She pulled on a sweater, navy blue, and went out for a walk since she'd missed one that morning. After ten minutes, she felt calm enough to laugh out loud. This was really about Georgia. She probably rolled her eyes at everyone. Narcissists were like that.

Still, she'd felt better about herself and her mother before the treatments. Now she wondered if Georgia's selfishness in leaving them had been the reason Jolene was so insecure and needy—which had led her to join a cult. And Rox was no longer sure she wanted to be more like everyone else. Being emotionally aware was rather painful. But maybe she just needed time to adjust and evaluate. She stopped walking, found the clinic listing in her cell phone, and left a message asking to reschedule her next treatment. It would be better to wait until she'd completed Emma's extraction and had more time to see how she handled the changes without the pressure of an intense case. Feeling better—and hungry now—Rox headed home.

In the kitchen, she pulled a container of spaghetti sauce from the freezer, dumped it in a pan, and turned on the stove. She always made a big batch and froze it for several dinners, usually inviting Marty, who'd taught her how to make it. When he came over, she cooked vermicelli to go with it, but alone, she spooned it up like chili.

While the sauce heated, she turned on the news. After ten minutes of political bullshit, the newscaster, a cute older guy with whitish-gray hair, pulled his face into a sad expression. "Just hours ago, a body was found near the interstate just south of the 205 junction. Police have labeled the death a homicide and say the young woman could be another victim of the I-5 Killer. If so, she would be the fourth victim since October of last year. The task force is asking for the public's help to identify the victim. If you knew this woman or saw her anytime in the last twenty-four hours, please call this number." Next to the phone number, an image of the young woman was displayed on the screen. She had long ash-colored hair and a chubby face.

Rox sucked in her breath. It was Bethany, the girl she'd chatted with at the soup kitchen.

CHAPTER 10

Rox grabbed her phone and called Kyle. She didn't expect him to answer, but she planned to leave a message in case the task force hadn't identified Bethany yet. As his cell rang, she visualized herself sitting in the soup kitchen in a nun's habit, chatting with the murder victim hours before her death. *Oh hell.* The subsequent conversation with Kyle played out in her head too. *Not good.* Yet she had to tell him that Bethany was a member of Sister Love. Or had the task force already learned that? Maybe she should just hang up. Her chat with Bethany was probably irrelevant to the girl's murder and the I-5 Killer investigation. But she had to say something.

Kyle's voice mail greeting ended. She played her report down the middle. "Hey, I just saw the news about the new I-5 victim. I wanted you to know she's a member of Sister Love, the veterans' charity, and that she had worked in their soup kitchen. I know you guys are keeping busy with the case, but call me when you have time." Rox hung up. If Bethany had been murdered by the serial killer, the I-5 team would focus on that lead. Maybe her own visit with Bethany would never come up. *Fat chance.* Kyle was a good detective, and he would ask a lot of questions. Rox decided she would be honest about her visit to the soup kitchen but not mention the costume. That involved too much explanation. Kyle would also want to question Deacon Blackstone.

What if Bethany wasn't an I-5 victim? Blackstone had a history of violence and could have killed the girl himself. But with what motive?

Five options popped into Rox's head, with the most prominent that he'd sexually assaulted Bethany and she'd threatened to report him. Rox got up and paced between the living room and kitchen, her thoughts spinning. With the police investigating the cult, her chance of extracting Emma was seriously jeopardized. Could she persuade Kyle, or any member of the task force, to look for Emma while they were out at the compound? Rox really wanted to tag along. Maybe they would even let her. Not likely. This wasn't TV.

A familiar knock made her turn to the front of the house. "Clear."

Marty bustled through the door. "Did you see the news? The I-5 Killer got another one." He'd never worked the homicide beat, but he diligently followed important police investigations.

Rox gestured toward the kitchen, and he followed her. She pulled two dark beers from the fridge and handed him one. "The victim's name is Bethany. She's a Sister Love member, and I talked to her yesterday at the soup kitchen."

Marty's mouth dropped open. "No kidding? Did you call Kyle and report it?"

"Sort of." She opened her brew and took a long swallow. "I didn't mention that I'd talked to Bethany because I was wearing a nun's habit and calling myself Sister Helen at the time."

"Oh shit." Marty sat down. "If anyone reports that conversation, they may look for you."

"They might even consider me a suspect."

Marty took a sip of beer, paused for a moment, then shook his head. "No, they'll focus on her last twenty-four hours, and a nun in a soup kitchen isn't a red flag."

"But we don't know when she was killed. If it happened last night, my chat with Bethany will be in the window of suspects."

"That depends on how many people they have to question."

They drank in silence. As ex-cops, they both knew the process and mind-set of those working the case. Rox finally said, "It also depends on how heavily they focus on a link to the I-5 Killer. If the news reported a connection, then the MO has to be similar."

"The girl fits the type. Young, long hair, not connected to her family." Marty gave her a look. "What are you thinking? That Blackstone did it? Made it look like the serial killer?"

"It's possible."

"Motive?"

"Covering up sexual abuse or something similar. They need to question Blackstone." A dark thought crossed her mind. "What if the task force doesn't know where to find him?" Rox couldn't sit any longer. She wanted to be at the Portland Police Bureau, facilitating the investigation. She loved hunting the bad guys. Why had she ever quit law enforcement? Oh right, because they always stuck her at a desk. She stood and put her beer back in the fridge. "I'm going down to the department. The I-5 team is working out of the central building. Some detectives will be at the crime scene, but others are probably in a meeting right now."

Marty jumped up. "I'm going with you."

He wouldn't like this. "I think I'll do better on my own. Having both of us try to get involved will seem obnoxious. And I have a natural connection with Kyle."

Marty's eyes narrowed. "You're probably right." He grabbed his beer. "Promise you'll keep me updated. And text me if you can't talk."

She almost laughed. Six months ago, he wouldn't have known how to read a text. "I will. And if you don't hear from me, then I've been detained, and you'd better come down and fight to get me out."

He laughed. "That depends on how high they set your bail."

A light rain fell as she parked near the PPB headquarters on Second Avenue. She'd worked a data desk out of this building for years, but after her stint in the CIA, it seemed a lifetime ago.

Before getting out of the car, she called Kyle again, mostly as a courtesy. She didn't want him to feel blindsided by her involvement. She left another message: "I'm at the central building, and I'm going in to tell the task force what I know about Bethany and the Sister Love cult leader." That made it sound like she had real information. "Which is not much," she added at the last moment.

Rox pulled her hood over her head and hurried down the block and inside the building. She crossed the lobby, noticing a young woman with two children waiting in the corner. She probably had a husband or boyfriend being questioned in a closet-like interrogation room. As Rox approached the plastic-glass counter, the uniformed officer looked up. Was that a tiny smile at the corner of his mouth? Rox glanced down to see if she'd rushed out of the house in pajamas again. Nope. She looked up and forced herself to smile back. It couldn't hurt, whatever his reason was.

"I'm Roxanne MacFarlane. I worked for the Portland department for seven years, and now I'm a private investigator. I have information pertaining to the I-5 Killer case, and I'd like to speak with Detective Zahn." A sergeant was officially in charge of the task force, but Zahn was the senior detective. Kyle had been on the team for six months, and she'd heard plenty about the personalities of its members. Kyle liked and respected Zahn, so he seemed like the person to contact.

For a long moment, the desk clerk processed the information, his dark eyes unsure. Finally he said, "He's in a meeting, but I'll let him know you're here."

"Thank you. This could be important."

The officer pointed at the lobby. "Have a seat. This could take a moment."

Rox didn't move. "I'd rather wait here."

His jaw tightened, and he walked away.

Six minutes later, the desk officer was back. This time he pointed to a dark door next to the counter. "I'll buzz you in." She knew how the security worked but didn't say anything. The officer led her to a familiar conference room upstairs and opened the door. "Don't expect a warm welcome."

She understood the attitude toward civilian interference, but it annoyed her anyway. Rox stepped into the room. Five men and one woman sat at a long table, all in casual business jackets. She didn't know any of them personally. She'd been away from the department for more than a decade and had never worked homicide when she was here. A tall man with close-cropped silver hair sat at one end, with a long whiteboard and a giant monitor behind him. From Kyle's descriptions, she assumed he was Detective Zahn. Rox walked directly over and offered her hand. "Rox MacFarlane."

Taken aback, the lead investigator gave her a weak handshake. "Michael Zahn. We're pretty busy here with a new homicide, so let's make this quick."

He hadn't asked her to sit down, but she felt uncomfortable standing. What was appropriate? She didn't care. Rox slid into the closest empty chair. "I'm a private investigator working a confidential case. I wanted to inform you that I talked to the newest victim yesterday afternoon. She was working in the Sister Love soup kitchen near Chinatown and told me her name is Bethany. I thought you would want to know."

"Do you know her last name?" Detective Zahn's tone softened.

"No, sorry. I really don't know anything about her. My case involves another young woman."

"You could have just called us with that information." An edge was back in his voice.

She had to steer them away from her encounter with Bethany. "I also know the location of the charity's home base. I thought it might be useful." She hesitated, not sure she wanted to send them in that direction. But she had to. "I mean, if you plan to question Deacon Blackstone, the leader."

Everyone at the table leaned forward. The heavyset detective across from her snapped, "Tell us what you know about Blackstone and why we should suspect him."

"I don't have any specific reason to think he killed Bethany. But he's a dirtbag who runs a questionable charity, and I believe the members all live with him." Rox turned back to Zahn, ignoring the fat jackass. "Does the evidence at the crime scene point to the I-5 Killer?"

"We can't share that."

"I worked at this department for seven years and spent a decade with the CIA. I can be trusted with confidential information." Plus, her stepdad spent thirty years with the department, and her boyfriend was on the task force. She kept that to herself for now.

A long silence.

She added, "The media already reported the link, so it's not exactly a secret."

Another moment of quiet. Finally Zahn asked, "What is your interest in Blackstone and his charity?"

"I'm looking for a young woman who might also be living at the compound."

"Do you suspect she's dead?"

A flash of dread in her gut. "It's possible. But I have no concrete reason to think that. I intend to find her one way or another."

Zahn drummed the table. "Do you have a good reason for not telling us her name?"

Well, yeah. Next week she might kidnap Emma, so it was best they didn't have proof of her connection to the girl. She hoped they would accept her other response. "Client confidentiality. Their names aren't relevant to your investigation."

"How do you know?" Zahn demanded. "What if your missing girl killed Bethany? They were both in the same organization. What if your clients killed her?"

Rox flushed, but held her ground. "The girl isn't strong enough to strangle anyone, and my clients just want their daughter back from the cult." They also wanted to know if she was still alive. Rox considered giving them Emma's name so they could check on her. But if they did, they might spook Emma and/or Blackstone. If the cult leader tucked Emma away deeper in the work camp, that would make an extraction even more difficult.

Before she could speak, the heavyset detective cut in. "If they run a soup kitchen, why do you call it a cult?"

Was he stupid or just looking for information? "Blackstone, the leader, is secretive. He also recruits vulnerable young women and depersonalizes them by confiscating their worldly possessions. All classic signs of a cult." But none of that by itself made Blackstone a killer. Still, cult leaders often had suicidal tendencies and didn't hesitate to take everyone with them. They all felt like they owned their followers. "Will you answer my question about the scene of the crime?"

A brief hesitation. Then Zahn said, "It was another strangulation, so it looks like the I-5 Killer's MO, but we haven't processed the trace evidence yet, and our people are still investigating."

Rox decided to get out before they asked her more questions. She could ask Kyle to look for Emma at the work camp on the down-low, without the task force knowing. She would send him Emma's photo so he had something to go on. Rox stood. "Thanks. If you want to question Blackstone, I'm pretty sure he and his members are living in an abandoned work camp off Barton Road." She started to leave.

"How do you know that?" Zahn called out.

She shrugged. "I'm an investigator." Rox stepped toward the door again.

"Wait. We're not done here." Zahn used his authoritative voice, a skill that all cops learned in training.

Damn! Rox turned back. "There's nothing else to tell. I wasn't even sure this was important enough to bother you with." She tried to downplay the whole thing.

"You said you saw Bethany at the soup kitchen. What time?" Zahn stood to be at her level.

Double damn. This was turning into an interrogation. But she'd known the risk. "Around three thirty."

"Did you speak to her?"

"Briefly."

"About what?"

"The charity and why she joined. Social chitchat."

"What was your objective?"

"Just background information."

The door opened, and Kyle walked in with his partner behind him. Kyle did a double take when he saw her standing there. Rox nodded, then turned back to Detective Zahn. "I have to go. Best wishes with this case." She hurried out, catching Kyle's eye on the way.

Behind her, she heard him say, "Excuse me for a moment." Kyle followed her into the hall, where she waited.

"What are you doing here?"

She couldn't read the expression on his face, but her best guess was worry.

"I called you several times and left messages." Rox took a quick breath. "Short version: the case I'm working involves Sister Love, and the murdered girl is one of the cult's members. But if this is an I-5 case, none of that might be important." Rox took out the small photo of Emma and showed it to him. "This is my clients' daughter. If you get inside Blackstone's complex, please check on her. The parents need to know she's alive."

He hesitated, and his brow furrowed. "If I can."

"Thanks. Call me after your meeting. Or just come over."

He shrugged. "If it's not too late." Kyle touched her arm, then hurried back into the conference room.

Was he annoyed at the involvement? She would have loved to follow him in, sit in a corner, and listen to them talk about the case and

Blackstone in particular. But she would have to settle for whatever crumbs Kyle could share. She thought about the Sister Love girls at the truck stop and wondered if she should have mentioned the scene. If she had, Zahn might send cops out there to shut it down. Which could be a good thing. But right now, she needed more information, and talking to the cult members seemed like the best way to get it. Rox decided she would drive to the truck stop and see if she could find the cult crew. Maybe pull one of the girls aside and question her. It was time to step up the extraction timeline. Emma could be in serious danger.

CHAPTER 11

Friday, April 21, 5:15 a.m.

Emma woke to an odd sound outside and opened her eyes, startled. Then she remembered it was the damn rooster! She'd never heard the sound in real life until she'd moved here. She'd never milked a cow or picked vegetables from a garden either. She'd learned to accept all of it and even liked the gardening stuff, but at the moment, she missed her old bed. It was bigger, softer, and so much prettier. She sat up and reached for her clothes. Her whole life growing up had been softer. No real chores, money to shop and play with, eating in fancy restaurants with her parents. She realized now how privileged she'd been. Not just privileged—spoiled. Nobody needed that many clothes or gadgets or meals that cost thirty dollars for a skinny plate of food. But right now, she wanted a cute T-shirt and a pretty pair of earrings to put on.

Emma yanked on the plain blue scrubs, grateful they were at least comfortable and not a horrible color like yellow. Not that clothes or colors mattered. All she needed was peace of mind and a life of service. Warm tears rolled down her cheeks, and she brushed them aside. She had nothing to cry about. Marlee's parents had something to cry about. They shed tears every day for the daughter they'd lost. She could still hear Mrs. Kramer screaming, her face distorted by grief and hate and soaked with tears. *You ruined my life! And I'll never forgive you! You don't deserve to live!* Emma had taken that to heart and almost killed herself before finding Sister Love. But now she had let that thought go. Her life could still have purpose, but all she could do was atone.

She looked around her screened-off section of the long doom room. A bed with a plain gray blanket, a small beat-up dresser, and a fresh drawing pad with colored pencils. Deacon had bought them for her last week after kissing her for the first time. She'd been surprised but pleased by his affection. She wasn't sure she'd earned the privilege of making art, and even if she had, she wasn't inspired. She was afraid she would end up with a page full of wrecked cars and dead bodies.

Emma pushed back the heavy curtain and stepped out. Jewel had just come out of her space and greeted her with a sad "Good morning."

Oh right, she had been close to Bethany, who had taken off without saying good-bye. Emma silently hugged her. Fresh tears rolled down Emma's face as she walked to the public-style bathroom with multiple toilets and sinks. This had been a jail long ago, and it suited the girls here. They were all prisoners of their guilt.

After brushing her teeth, she headed to the kitchen to brew coffee and start breakfast. What else would today bring? *Another blood donation,* she remembered. Emma cringed. Maybe she would get a private moment with Deacon. She didn't deserve his love, but she wanted it. She wasn't really ready for sex, but if he thought it was good for her, then she would go along. She needed the attention, the closeness. Something to keep the darkness at bay.

Later, after the kitchen was clean, Emma headed for Margo's office, her stomach queasy. She knocked, said her name, then entered. Margo was expecting her.

"You had protein for breakfast, right?" Margo pulled on latex gloves as she spoke.

"Yes. I feel a little queasy though."

"I'm surprised this still makes you nervous." Margo smiled. "You'll be fine. Have a seat, please."

Emma eased into the leather recliner and leaned back. The medical tray with blood-draw equipment was now at eye level, and her stomach tightened. None of the other sisters seemed to mind giving blood, but she hated needles. *Get over it,* she told herself. This was lifesaving. She owed this to the universe.

Margo started scrubbing the inside crook of Emma's elbow with yellow iodine. "We might have a new member joining us soon. Her name is Celine, and I'm counting on you to make her feel welcome."

"Of course I will." Was Margo singling her out or just chatting to distract her?

Margo wrapped Emma's upper arm, handed her a spongy ball, and told her to start squeezing. When the needle came toward her, Emma looked away and braced.

"Relax, or it will hurt."

Emma forced herself to think about cute kittens. The stick of the needle was the worst of it, but even after, she couldn't look at the sight of blood flowing from her body. She'd made that mistake the first time and passed out. She watched Margo put away the medical supplies. It was odd that Margo was a CNA, yet she was the only woman at Sister Love who didn't wear scrubs. But Margo had to wear them at the hospital, so Emma didn't blame her for not wanting to wear them at home. And Margo didn't have anything to atone for. Emma and her sisters wore the scrubs as a sacrifice, to deny themselves the pleasure of pretty clothes. Emma squeezed the sponge ball in her hand again, trying to fill the bag as fast as she could.

When she was almost done, the door opened, and Deacon stepped into the room. He nodded at Margo. "Wrap this up." Then he turned to Emma. "When you're done here, come to my office."

Emma nodded.

Margo shook her head. "She needs another minute to make a complete pint. My contact might not buy a partial." She spoke through gritted teeth.

They sold the blood? Emma had assumed they donated it to hospitals. She kept quiet. The charity needed money to operate and feed people, and the blood still went to a good cause.

"Fine." Deacon stepped back out of the room.

Emma squeezed the little ball harder, and a few minutes later, a tiny bell sounded, indicating the blood bag had hit its full weight.

"Good girl." Margo came over, pulled out the needle, and wrapped pressure tape around the tiny wound.

But she didn't offer her a cookie, like last time. Emma was disappointed—they got so few treats—but spending time alone with Deacon was better than a cookie. "See you later." Emma gave Margo a friendly smile and hurried out, then strode down the hall.

She knocked on Deacon's door, and he pulled it open, as if waiting for her. When she stepped in, he touched her cheek. "How are you doing?"

"I'm sad about Bethany leaving, but I'm holding on to my peace of mind."

"Good girl." He hugged her with one arm and led her to the couch. "We have something important to talk about."

A shiver ran up her spine. She was curious, but she resisted the urge to sound eager. "Okay."

"The charity is in trouble. We're running out of cash, and we need a couple of large donations or we might have to shut down."

"No! We can't let that happen." But she was confused. "How can I help?"

"You need to contact your parents and ask them to make a significant contribution."

What? "But you said no contact with loved ones."

"I know. This is an exception to save Sister Love. And you're strong enough to handle it."

She didn't feel strong. Just the sound of her mother's voice would make her homesick. Emma shook her head. "They will never give money to the charity. They don't want me here."

"But they do want to see you." His eyes pleaded with her. "Tell them if they donate ten thousand dollars, you'll get to meet with them for an hour."

Emma was taken aback. Her parents had that kind of money, but it felt wrong. "I'm not sure about this. What if they call the police?"

"And say what? We're a charity. We ask everyone for money." He gave her a charming smile. "Except the veterans we serve."

"But it feels like a bribe or something." *Was that the right word?*

"It's not. It would just be a donation, followed by a family get-together. After a year, you were going to earn a visitation anyway." Deacon leaned in, kissed her softly, and whispered, "You've earned it."

Oh god, that felt good. Emma kissed him back, hungry for his affection.

But he pulled away. "You have to make the call. Do this for your sisters. So I don't have to put them out on the streets where they'll do drugs to forget their pain." His eyes locked on hers. "Or kill themselves. Remember how you felt out there on your own?"

She couldn't let any of that happen. "All right."

"Good girl." He jumped up and grabbed a cell phone from his desk.

Disappointed to be done kissing, Emma braced herself. She hadn't talked to her mother in four months. This might make them both cry. She hated the thought. She used to not care much about her mother's feelings, but she did now.

Deacon handed her the cell. "Keep it brief. Tell her the meeting will be in a public place of our choosing."

Her old phone! She had turned it over to Deacon when she'd moved into the Sister Love complex. Even though she didn't need it, she was happy he still had it.

"Tell her she has only until the end of the day to decide. Put the phone on speaker and make the call."

Emma pressed the familiar icon. After three rings, a familiar high-pitched voice said, "Emma?"

"Hey, Mom."

"Oh my god!" Her mother burst into tears. "It's so good to hear your voice. Are you okay?"

Just breathe. "Yes. I have a request." Emma struggled to control her own emotions while she waited for her mother to calm down. "My charity needs help. We need you to donate ten thousand dollars." She choked on the words.

"Are you kidding?" Her mother went from sad to mad in three seconds. "Why would I help the bastard who stole you from me? The bastard who won't let me see you?"

It wasn't like that, but there was no point in trying to explain. "If you make the donation, you will get to see me."

"Really? For how long?" Hope and eagerness now.

"An hour. In a public place."

A long pause. "So this is a shakedown. Ten grand for an hour of your time?"

Emma cringed. She'd known it was wrong. "I'm sorry. But we need the money to keep the charity going."

Her mother let out a harsh laugh. "I have no interest in keeping the charity going. If the damn thing folds up, you'll come home to me."

Emma hadn't thought of that. From the look on Deacon's face, he hadn't either. She decided to be honest. "Even if the charity closes, I won't come home. I can't ever go back to my old life. I don't deserve it."

"You have to stop punishing yourself!" Her mother was crying again.

Deacon gestured at her to wrap it up.

"I have to go. You have only today to make the donation. Bye, Mom." Emma started to close the call, then blurted out, "I love you." Tears rolled down her face as she hung up.

"You handled that well." Deacon kissed her cheek. "She'll call back and offer us the money."

Abruptly the door burst open, and Ronnie stepped in. "The police are here."

CHAPTER 12

Deacon strode down the wide hall over the scarred industrial floor. He spotted Skeeter watching him from a broom closet and snapped at her, "Go to your room and stay there for a while." The skinny, freckled girl scampered off. Most of the members were in the main dorm, a separate building out back. He didn't have time to coach them about what to say if the officers wanted to question everyone. But he had no intention of letting cops inside without a warrant. Deacon took a calming breath. The girls were all eighteen or older, and they lived here of their own free will. He had no reason to be worried and nothing to hide.

Well, almost nothing. They didn't have an FDA license to draw blood, and their client sold the plasma on the black market to stem-cell researchers. The thought of being arrested gave him a jolt. Once he was out from under the care-center payments, they would stop the blood draws. He wanted to be completely legit—and never see the inside of a jail again.

Deacon stopped at the wide front door and glanced at the monitor. Two men in dark suits stood on the narrow cement step, looking impatient. Deacon spoke into the intercom. "Who are you, and what do you want?"

On the small screen, he saw them glance around for the speaker and camera. The taller man said, "Detective Wilson and Detective Stewart with the Portland Police Bureau. Are you Deacon Blackstone?"

"Yes. What do you want?"

"We'd like to ask you a few questions. Can we come in?"

"Questions about what?"

"A girl named Bethany."

Oh shit. This was trouble. But at least they weren't looking for Emma. "What about Bethany?"

"We'd like to come inside and speak with you in person."

"Do you have a warrant?"

"No, but we can get one."

Easier said than done and likely a bluff. But it was better to just deal with this now. "I'll come out." Deacon pressed the small buzzer, leaned against the push-bar handle, and stepped outside. The brightness of the morning surprised him. He'd been so preoccupied with finding donations, he hadn't left the building since Wednesday or noticed the weather.

Even the taller of the two detectives was shorter than him, and Deacon outweighed him by thirty pounds of muscle. Always an advantage to be the biggest man. "What's going on with Bethany?"

"What's her last name?"

"I think it's Grant, but the members don't use last names here."

An eye roll from Detective Wilson. "When did you see her last?"

A stab of worry hit Deacon. "Wednesday, around seven. I hear she left the property sometime later that night. I know I haven't seen her since."

"Where were you Wednesday evening between nine and midnight?"

They were treating him like a suspect! "Driving home. I visited my father at the Linnwood Care Facility and got home around eleven." He had to ask. "Why? Did something happen to Bethany?"

"She was murdered." The detective's expression was unflinching. "Did anyone see you arrive home that night?"

This shit was getting deeper. "How was Bethany killed?"

"Answer my question."

No one had seen him come in. Margo had been at work, the night-crew girls had still been out, and the soup kitchen girls had gone to bed. He had to handle this just right. "People at the nursing home can vouch for when I left." Deacon reached in his pocket for a cigarette and lit up, feeling instantly better.

"We'd like to question everyone who lives here." The tall detective, Wilson, was still taking the lead.

"That's completely unnecessary. We're a charitable foundation. The members are good-hearted people. None of them had anything to do with Bethany's death." Deacon let his concern show, a rare display of emotion for him.

"We'd like to establish a timeline." The detective took out a notepad. "Knowing when Bethany left here may help us determine where she went and who she saw."

"I've already asked the members, and no one saw her leave. But I'll ask again. If anyone has information, I'll pass it along." Deacon took a drag, wanting to wrap up the conversation. This was such a waste of time. "You're looking in the wrong place. The only contact our members have with the outside world is to run a soup kitchen for veterans and occasionally solicit donations. Please leave the property now." He started to step back toward the door.

The detective grabbed his arm, then quickly let go. "Do you own this land?"

"No. I lease it from Charles Zumwalt." Deacon had met Zumwalt at the senior facility where his dad had lived before he needed full-time care. When Zumwalt mentioned the land and empty buildings he owned, Deacon had seen an opportunity and worked out a deal. They paid almost nothing for rent. It was the rich old guy's way of contributing to a veterans' cause—and getting some young-thing action as a bonus.

"We'll be back with a warrant," Wilson announced, sounding confident.

"To search for what?"

"We need to see Bethany's personal belongings and check her cell phone and computer to see who she contacted."

Deacon let out a laugh. "Sister Love members don't have cell phones or any personal items. They leave it all behind when they join and devote their lives to service."

Frustration flashed in the detective's eyes. "No computer either then?"

"No." Deacon realized he hadn't expressed any grief, and it probably didn't look good. "I loved Bethany. We all did. She was safe here. But she decided to leave, and whatever happened to her out there has nothing to do with us."

The shorter detective cut in. "Is there any reason you don't want us to come in and look around?" His tone was accusatory.

Because you're a dick. Deacon gave him a nasty smile. "I'm a private person, and the Sister Love members are all wounded souls. Your presence here is already disturbing, and now I have to tell them that Bethany is dead." Deacon honestly dreaded the chore. He'd done enough of it in his military service tours. "I hope you find her killer." He dropped his cigarette, stepped inside, and slammed the door. Deacon watched on the monitor as the detectives chatted about what to do next. The tall one held up a business card and pushed it through the mail slot near the door. They both turned and walked away. Deacon grabbed the card off the floor and hurried to his office, where he planned to watch out the window to make sure they drove off.

Ronnie was lurking in the hall and called out, "What's going on?"

Why wasn't she at the soup kitchen? Her day off? He ignored her question. "Wait ten minutes, then gather everyone in the dining hall." Deacon kept moving. Margo's daughter annoyed the hell out of him, but he hadn't figured out how to get rid of her. Yet. She'd been fun when she was younger, but her drug addiction while she was on the streets had ruined her looks, and now she was too old and fat. In the meantime,

Ronnie helped keep the girls in line. He reached his office in time to see the dark sedan exit the gravel parking area and head back toward town.

Breathing a sigh of relief, Deacon sat down to gather his thoughts. He would get through this. The girls would keep quiet about the blood draws, and if the police ever got a subpoena to look at the charity's financials, they would be disappointed. He and Margo dealt in cash as much as they could. But would the police find Bethany's money? As far as Deacon knew, he and Margo had the only paperwork relating to her trust account. Without it, no one would ever know—unless the California bank informed them. The two grand in the account wasn't enough to fix his money problems, but it would help—if they could find a way to access it without Bethany. And the royalties should keep coming.

He'd targeted the girl online a few months after her incident. Alone in the world after accidentally shooting her father, she'd been eager to join Sister Love. But Deacon wouldn't contact the bank about the trust until the police investigation died down. So now wasn't the time to think about it. He had to deal with the members first. He shut off his password-protected computer and headed for the dining hall.

The chatter in the room surprised him at first, then he remembered the girls didn't know about Bethany yet. They quieted down as soon as he entered. Margo wasn't present, and he wondered if Ronnie had even asked her to join them. But his girlfriend came in a moment later and strode over to him.

"What's going on?" she whispered.

He should have told her first, but it was too late for that. "It's bad news, and I have to tell everyone."

Deacon scanned the room. Everyone was accounted for, except the four sisters at the soup kitchen. And Bethany, of course. He would have to step up his recruitment efforts, but he still had to be selective. He wasn't impressed with Celine, a twenty-year-old that Margo was working. The charity had delicate intake-output equilibrium, and more members could mean more expenses—unless they came with resources or would be good at working the truck stops. Unfortunately finding girls with money was challenging.

"Sisters, I have some bad news." Deacon tried to think of a way to soften the news but couldn't. "The cops were just here to inform me that Bethany was killed Wednesday night after she left us. I don't know anything else. The detectives wouldn't tell me how or why."

Deacon waited as the members gasped in shock and cried out "No!" and "Oh my god." Within a minute, most of the girls were crying. Ronnie stood and started to leave the room, then changed her mind. She was clearly upset but trying to keep herself together. Margo was moving from girl to girl, hugging them. The emotion in the room was overwhelming, and Deacon desperately wanted out. But he had to ask questions and show the cops that he was being cooperative.

Deacon raised his voice to be heard over the sobbing. "The police need your help. I know I asked this yesterday when I found out Bethany was gone, but it's even more important now. Did anyone see her leave?"

No one responded.

"Does anyone know why she left or where she was going?"

The crying continued. He tried again, nearly shouting. "If you know anything, please come forward. Otherwise, the police will be back with a search warrant and question all of you."

Jewel, Emma, and Ronnie all looked up.

Jewel got up and came toward him, head down. "I think I know. I'm sorry I didn't tell you." Her big eyes were wild with grief and worry.

The poor girl had been Bethany's best friend. Deacon gently touched her shoulder. "What do you know?"

"I didn't see Bethany leave that night, so I didn't lie. But I've seen her leave before. I think she was visiting a boy who lives near Barton Road."

Rage filled Deacon's chest, and he couldn't speak. Bethany was *his* girl! How dare she cheat on him with some pip-squeak kid. Just because he'd lost interest in her sexually, that didn't give her the right to fuck someone else.

"Please don't be mad at me." Jewel looked terrified.

"I'm not. Who is this boy, and how do you know she was seeing him?"

"I don't know his name, but he's often near the creek when the van drives by on the way to the soup kitchen. They waved at each other all the time, and once, she dropped a note out the window."

Deacon had dealt with this once before, a girl named Jaylene who'd finally left the charity. One of the few who had. Most of them would age out eventually, and that was fine. They were harder to control as they got older and less desirable. "Do you know his name or where he lives?"

"No."

He didn't need the information; the police did. Once the cops had a new suspect, he hoped to hell they would leave him and his girls alone. His anger subsided. Bethany had paid for her disloyalty with her life, and he was tired of her anyway. But Emma was still a ripe peach, ready for picking. He gestured at Jewel. "Come with me to call the police. They need to know about her boyfriend."

He hurried toward his office, eager to get this bullshit over with. He hadn't spent any time in the greenhouse yet today, and it was making him edgy. Need was his constant companion. Food, sex, stimulation— he constantly craved something. But the greenery and damp lushness of the garden always soothed him. For a while. As a kid, he'd often escaped his father's angry fist by hiding in the public gardens near their house. As a troubled teenager, he'd been assigned to work in those gardens, learning to grow food. Much of the fresh produce had been donated to local soup kitchens, an idea that had stuck with him.

Jewel lagged behind, and he waited for her at the office door. "Hurry up."

"I don't want to talk to the police." Tears trickled down her face.

"You want to help find Bethany's killer, don't you?" Deacon was surprised by his patience with her.

"Yes, but I'm nervous." She pressed her lips together. "I doubt if that boy killed her. He's just a kid."

"We'll let the detectives decide that." Deacon stepped aside and let Jewel enter first. He pulled his cell phone out of the top drawer, hesitating to use it. But he had to get a new one soon anyway. Deacon keyed in the number from the detective's card and focused on Jewel. "Just tell them what you know about Bethany's contact with the neighbor boy."

The door opened, and Margo stepped in. "What's happening now?"

Deacon held up his hand to silence her. "We're calling the police. Jewel saw Bethany sneak out to see a local boy."

Margo looked skeptical and worried. "What if she was murdered by the I-5 Killer? The rest of our girls could be in danger."

CHAPTER 13

Friday, April 21, 9:25 a.m.

At the kitchen table, Rox sipped coffee and read through her notes on the case, unsure of what to do next. Bethany's murder changed everything. If Blackstone had killed her, the timetable for Emma's extraction would need to be compressed. Even if he hadn't, the I-5 Killer probably had, and the psycho might target more Sister Love girls. She remembered the person she'd seen lurking at the truck stop. He was probably harmless, maybe even an undercover cop. But still, Rox wasn't worried just about Emma. All the other young women in the charity were vulnerable too. But why would Blackstone risk everything to murder one of his members? If he was guilty, his motive had to be about money—unless it was a spontaneous crime of passion. Maybe Bethany had spurned him sexually, and he lost control?

On the other hand, if Bethany was a victim of the I-5 Killer, which seemed more likely, then maybe Rox still had time to plan a careful sting operation. Her burner phone rang in her pocket, startling her. Probably the Carsons. There wasn't much chance of landing another x-client already.

Rox hurriedly picked up, noticing she'd missed an earlier call from the same number. "Karina Jones."

"This is Jenny Carson." The woman sounded breathless. "Emma called me earlier this morning."

That was unexpected. "What did she say?"

"She asked us to donate ten thousand dollars to the charity. If we do, we supposedly get to see her for an hour. I don't know what I should do."

An opportunity! "We need to make this opening work for us. Let me think about when and where."

"I'm sure the bastard plans to be there and chaperone." Jenny's voice rose even higher. "How do we get Emma alone?"

"I'm working on that." Rox's first thought was Kyle. Maybe he could arrange for Blackstone to be picked up for questioning . . . just moments after Emma connected with her parents. Not easy, but doable. "I have contacts with the police, so I'll see what I can set up."

"There's more." Jenny's voice trembled with worry. "Did you see the paper this morning? A Sister Love member, a girl named Bethany, was murdered."

"I know. I'm worried too. But the police think Bethany was a victim of the I-5 Killer." She might as well put her client at ease.

A pause. "Blackstone only gave us until the end of the day to make up our minds about the donation, but I don't think Dave will go along. He'll say it's extortion or blackmail or something."

"Technically it's a bribe. But when it's between individuals and not government officials, it's not illegal. Did Blackstone ask for cash?"

"Yes."

"We'll have you bring the money and show it to him, but tell him he can't have it until you get your full hour." If Blackstone was picked up by police or somehow distracted, the Carsons could keep their ten grand. "Meet me at my office in an hour, and we'll call him back from there with a plan."

"Should I bring the cash to your office?"

"It can't hurt to have it ready."

Jenny let out a muffled cry. "I'm so worried about my little girl."

Rox felt a rush of empathetic pain. For a moment she couldn't think. Finally she said, "The police are probably at the compound right now, questioning Blackstone. So Emma is safe for the moment."

"Okay. I'll see you in an hour."

They both hung up, and Rox paced the house, visualizing places they could arrange to meet with Blackstone. She had to call Kyle. If she could get an officer to pick up the cult leader during the meeting, or at least pull him away, they might have a chance to grab Emma. A best-case scenario. Blackstone might have his own ideas about where to set up the meet. He might even bring his girlfriend for extra security.

She pressed Kyle's speed dial icon. Not surprised that he didn't answer, she left him a message. "Please call me right away. My client has an opportunity to get her daughter away from Blackstone, but I could use some police assistance." Where the hell was Kyle? At the work camp questioning Blackstone? Would he even listen to her message? He hadn't come over the night before, but she understood. Murder investigations were intense during the first few days, and she usually didn't see or hear from him when he took a new case. The serial killer task force was a unique situation, and she hoped her peripheral involvement would motivate him to at least call and ask what the hell she was talking about.

Time to get her partner over to brainstorm again. She texted Marty: *New developments in the case. Let's discuss.*

While she waited to hear from him, she called the Clackamas County office. Should she pretend to be a real estate buyer or just be honest? A clerk answered, and Rox went with the truth. "I'm a private investigator looking for a missing young woman. I believe she's living with a cult on a property that used to be owned by the county. A work camp that probably served as an alternative jail."

"How can I help you?"

"I need to know who owns the property and how to contact them, if possible."

"We don't usually do property searches, but you're welcome to come in and browse the archives yourself."

She'd expected that. "A young woman is missing, and her parents haven't seen her in months. Another young woman in the same cult was murdered two days ago." Rox paused to let the clerk absorb all that. "I have to find the girl now, and I need your help."

A pause. "What's the address?"

"I'm not exactly sure. It's on a dead-end lane that has no sign. It's off Barton Road, about seven miles from Highway 212." Rox sat down at her computer and opened Google Maps. "I'm checking the location right now. I should have a street number in a moment." She'd asked Marty to find the owner, but then they'd heard about Bethany and got sidetracked.

"Maybe you should call back when you're ready."

"Hang on, I've got it." Rox zoomed in on the address Google displayed on the short lane labeled "Hamm," then read the long number out loud.

The clerk gave an exasperated sigh. "Give me a minute."

"Thanks."

While she waited, Rox checked her phone. No missed calls or texts. The familiar knock on the front door made her smile. Marty. She called out, "Clear," and he came in, looking sharp in a new T-shirt and black pants.

"You've been clothes shopping!"

"So?"

"You hate shopping as much as I do."

"You've never noticed my clothes before." Marty grinned. "That treatment must be working."

Had she never commented on his appearance? Really? Another thought hit her. "Are you dating that woman you met at the swing dance club?"

Another shy smile. "Maybe."

"I want to hear about it, but not now." Rox pointed at her earpiece. "I'm on hold with the county, so help yourself to some coffee."

The clerk took another three minutes, and Marty behaved himself by not bugging her until she was off the phone. Rox hung up and turned to him. "The owner of the work camp land is Charles Zumwalt. Can you track him down? Even if he can't help us get Emma out, he should at least know what's happening on his property."

"Maybe he does know." A lifelong cop, Marty didn't give anyone credit they hadn't earned. He grabbed her grocery list off the fridge and wrote down the owner's name. "Sorry I didn't get this done yesterday. I called the county and had to leave a message."

"No problem, but leave me the top half of that, please."

He glanced at her grocery list. "Cereal and toilet paper. I think you can remember that."

She laughed and sat down at the kitchen table again. Her coffee was cold now. "We need a plan."

He took a seat across from her. "We should sand and refinish this table, but give me the updates first."

Was that a wink? "Emma called her mother and asked her to donate ten grand to the charity."

Marty whistled. "Holy moley!"

"In exchange, the Carsons get to see their daughter for an hour."

"That's harsh. Do they have that kind of money?"

"Yeah, they're loaded. But we're not going to actually let Blackstone have the cash." Rox tapped her stepdad's hand. "This is where I might need your help. If I can't get Kyle to pick up Blackstone during the meet, then I need a uniform to pull him aside or detain him somehow. If I can just get some alone time with Emma, I think I can convince her to leave the cult."

"I'll ask Bowman. When and where is this meet set up?"

"We're not sure yet, so let me talk to Kyle first. Blackstone is a suspect in his case, so Kyle will be upset if I don't loop him in."

"Roger that." Marty shifted, looking eager to get moving. "You said *developments*. What else have you got?"

"Maybe that's it." She had called Marty right after her meeting with the task force the night before, so he just needed the morning news.

"Did you drive out to the truck stop after we talked last night?"

"Yeah, but I didn't find the crew. I knew that was likely; I was just too hyper to come home."

"I'm ready to move forward too. Blackstone and his whole operation give me the heebie-jeebies."

"He's a sneaky predator." Rox shivered. "I prefer bad guys who don't try to hide who they are."

"You and me both." Marty took his coffee cup to the sink. "What's next?"

Oh hell. She had to get going. Rox jumped up. "I'm meeting Jenny Carson at the office. She's going to call Blackstone and set up the rendezvous with Emma."

"Okay. I'll run down the landowner and wait to hear from you." Marty saluted and headed out.

Twenty minutes later, Rox pulled in behind her work building, relieved she hadn't seen Jenny Carson's white Mercedes in the front parking lot. She hurried into her interior office, hoping to keep her client in the lobby. She wanted to stay anonymous, if she could. But if any case would make her break the rule and risk being charged, it was this one. A jury would be as disgusted by Blackstone as she was.

Rox stood at her desk. On the way over, she'd decided the meeting should be someplace with crowds to blend into but also with pockets of private spaces. She assumed Blackstone would be thinking the same thing. A coffee shop inside a mall maybe? The front office bell sounded, and she glanced at the monitor. Jenny Carson stood at the door, looking classy in a black belted sweater—but worried too. In addition to the clutch purse in her hand, she wore a satchel strapped across her chest. Good, she had the cash with her. Now they just needed Blackstone to cooperate. Rox buzzed her in, suddenly irritated that Kyle hadn't called her back.

"Hi, Jenny. Have a seat." A wave of self-consciousness rolled over her, and Rox felt compelled to apologize. "I'm sorry we can't meet face-to-face, but it's to protect both of us." She realized she was getting too emotional about this case and needed to step back. She might not succeed in bringing Emma home. Or the girl might run right back to the cult. Blackstone's charity might be perfectly legal and keep chugging right along either way.

"I understand." Mrs. Carson sat down and pulled out her phone.

"Tell him you want to meet at Joey's Coffee near Waterfront Park."

Jenny's lips trembled as she pressed the keys. While she waited, the pretty woman looked up at the monitor. "They called from Emma's phone. I was overjoyed to see that they still have it."

But Blackstone might toss it after today. He was smart and careful. "Put him on speaker, please." She would send Jenny texts if she needed to communicate with her privately.

"I did." She placed her cell on the little desk.

Her client tensed as Blackstone's voice came through. "Are you making a donation?"

"Yes. And I have the cash."

"Great. Meet us at the Lotus Blossom in the Lloyd Center Mall in one hour."

"But my husband needs—"

Blackstone had hung up.

"Shit." They both said it at the same time.

The bastard was crafty too. "This is too fast," Rox said. "I need time to get a police officer involved."

"And Dave needs more advance warning. He's a busy man. But I'll call him and see if he can get away from his meetings." Jenny called her husband, then stood and walked toward the door.

She wanted privacy. Rox didn't hear their conversation, but when her client turned back, her brow was furrowed. She was pissed.

"Everything all right?"

"He can't be there." Jenny's mouth tightened. "His loss. He won't get to see our girl."

"We'd better go." Rox pulled on her sweater. "I'll keep out of sight. But I want a good look at Blackstone if nothing else. And I'll make another call and try to get an officer to pull him aside so I can move in and talk to Emma."

"I hate doing this without Dave." Jenny sounded scared.

"You're going to see your daughter. It's a positive development." Rox needed her to be confident. "This is a concession for him. Blackstone's need for money gives us leverage, a foot in the door." Rox smiled, then remembered her client couldn't see her through the pixilation. "Don't worry. I'll be nearby, watching. I've had extensive physical training, both as a police officer and federal agent. You'll be safe."

"I'm not afraid of Deacon Blackstone. I'm afraid Emma will walk away from me again."

Rox didn't know what to say.

CHAPTER 14

Rox got on the phone with Marty while walking to her car. "Hey, we need a uniform at the Lotus Blossom in the Lloyd Center Mall one hour from now. Can you make that happen?"

"I'll do my best. I've already tried Bowman, but he's on duty, so not likely taking personal calls. But if I keep trying, he might get curious. I'll try Foster too. But that may be it. A lot of my old partners have retired."

"I know. It's a big favor."

"I'll be there as backup." Marty made a throaty noise. "If we can't get an on-duty cop, do you want me to step in and try something? You know, bump into Blackstone and see if I can trigger a reaction. Maybe draw him away?"

She briefly considered it. "No. I think he's too slick and potentially violent. He might not even respect a uniformed officer."

"I'll just keep him in sight and be on standby to assist with the girl."

Would Marty try something anyway? "Hey, don't be a hero. If today doesn't work, we'll still try a safe extraction, with Blackstone out of the way."

"Roger that."

They hung up, and Rox drove toward downtown, her heart accelerating as wild scenarios played out in her mind. Fantasies in which Blackstone tried to take the money and run or got aggressive and she had to drive a fist into his throat. She'd been wanting to hurt someone ever since her sister had died. Three months of hitting a bag at the gym hadn't taken much of the edge off, so she'd started her business to put her anger to productive use. Still, she would have to control herself around Blackstone. Assaulting him could blow the case entirely and drive Emma deeper into his clutches. The last thing they needed was for the girl to perceive Blackstone as a victim.

The drive took only twenty minutes, but getting parked in the tall garage sucked up another ten. By the time she approached the mall, Jenny Carson was already seated at a little table just outside the restaurant door. Her client glanced around anxiously as Rox hurried by, head down, staring at her phone. She stepped into the store next door and turned back to watch, staying near the door. How long could she pretend to look at hats before the clerk got nervous and started hovering?

A few minutes later, a beefy, handsome man in a knit cap and denim jacket approached. Barely visible behind him was a scrawny girl with white-blonde hair. Rox couldn't see her face yet. The man was thick chested, with a strong jaw and wide-set eyes. But not totally Caucasian. She hadn't noticed his ethnicity in the small file photo. Was he half black? African Americans in Portland were so rare, they had their own website. None of that mattered. As the two people neared Mrs. Carson, the girl stepped out and let herself be seen. Her pale skin made her seem anemic, but Emma had her mother's classic rich-girl beauty: narrow nose, small mouth, and flawless skin.

Jenny and her daughter rushed toward each other and embraced. Pangs of joy and jealousy tugged at Rox's heart, but she stayed focused on Blackstone. He'd moved in, keeping himself within a foot of the girl. A moment later, he grabbed Emma's elbow and pulled her to his side. He said something to Mrs. Carson that Rox couldn't hear, then he and Emma turned and walked toward the street. Her client hurried to follow.

Where the hell were they going? Rox scooted out of the store, trying to look casual as she followed. This wasn't the plan. They were supposed to sit down and visit for an hour. But at least Blackstone hadn't taken the satchel full of cash and run, dragging Emma with him. Out of the corner of her eye, Rox saw a big MAX vehicle coming up the busy street. *No!* She quickened her pace, but the threesome was fifty feet ahead and moving rapidly. The bus stopped, and they climbed on behind a teenage boy. As Rox broke into a run, the door closed, and the bus lurched forward. *Damn!*

She noted the vehicle's route number, pulled out her phone, and called Marty. He picked up immediately. "What's happening?"

"Blackstone, Emma, and Mrs. Carson just got on a bus, headed down Multnomah. I didn't know how to stop them."

"Dammit. What's the bus number? Bowman's headed our way. Maybe he can intercept Blackstone when they get off."

"That could be anywhere. My client paid for an hour with her daughter, so they might ride for a while." She started toward her car.

"Or Blackstone might take the money and get off at the next stop."

Rox spun back around. No, she couldn't get there on foot in time, and her Cube's location was in the wrong direction. "Call Bowman, but I'm not optimistic."

She hung up and hurried to her car. There was probably nothing she could do now to improve the situation, but she would feel better if she were mobile and able to respond. Once she was on the street, Rox headed in the direction the bus had gone, hoping to hear something from Marty.

But they struck out. Twenty-five minutes after boarding the bus, Mrs. Carson called, audibly upset. "Sorry, but he said we had to do it his way." She pulled in a ragged breath. "He said I had to compromise and give him the money halfway through the visitation. So I did. And they jumped off at the next stop."

"Did you see which direction they went?"

"No. The bastard cheated me, but what can I do? I willingly made a donation to a charity." A small sob escaped her. "Dave is going to be mad."

Rox couldn't help her with that. "What did you and Emma talk about?"

"She asked about family and friends and how they were doing, so that took some time. And she told me a few things about her life in the charity."

Bowman hadn't made contact, so Rox made a turn, heading for home. "Like what? Anything helpful?"

"No. Just that she has kitchen duty and has learned to cook and garden." A pause. "She seems kind of happy, even at peace with herself."

That surprised Rox. "Are you having second thoughts about extracting her?"

"No. He's a predator, and my girl is too thin." Another stifled cry. "She also has bruises on her arms."

A flash of rage. "Did you ask her about them?"

"No. He was right there, listening to everything. I didn't want him to pull her away before my time was up."

"Don't worry. We'll get her out." Rox took a deep breath to calm herself. "We've located the owner of the land, and I'm plotting a way to get Blackstone away from the work camp long enough to go in and grab her."

"What if she just goes back?"

"That's what the deprogramming is for. But initially I think I can convince her to try another form of self-sacrifice." Rox didn't want to have this conversation yet. "I've got to get to work on plan B." She started to apologize for the failure of the meeting, then realized it wasn't her fault. She hadn't set it up and couldn't have done anything to change the outcome. "We'll be in touch."

◆ ◆ ◆

As she pulled into her driveway, her personal phone rang, and she answered without looking at the ID. "Hello."

"This is Denise, from the Greer Neurology Clinic. You had an appointment at two. Are you on your way?"

Damn! She'd completely lost track of it in the rush to meet Blackstone. Oh wait, she tried to cancel it. "I called yesterday and left a message saying I couldn't make it." She hoped they didn't bill her for it.

"Oh. I don't know what happened. We can reschedule for next week. Can you come in Wednesday, the twenty-sixth, at two?"

"Sure. Will you text me with a reminder?"

"We'll send an automated phone call the day before."

"Okay. Thanks." With any luck, this case would be over by then.

Rox shut off the car and hurried inside. She needed to pee and drink another cup of coffee—the fluid exchange. Before it finished brewing, Marty pounded on her door.

"Clear," she called from the kitchen.

He bustled in, scowling. "Pour me one too." He sat down and pulled off his Blazers cap. "I wonder how many other parents Blackstone has shaken down that way."

"Probably a few. But I doubt many can pony up ten grand."

"It's worth his time even for five hundred or a thousand."

Rox put both cups on the table and sat down. "But he can probably only get away with it once for each girl." She thought about Blackstone's recruitment tactics. "I wonder if he specifically targets young women with both guilt *and* family money."

Marty shook his head, his lip curled. "We need to close the door on this lowlife. Let's come up with a sting that rescues Emma and puts him out of business."

She'd been thinking the same thing. "I think it'll take too much time. Blackstone is careful. Let's just get the girl first, then work the second objective."

"Maybe we could offer him a donation." Marty shifted, and his eyes sparked with eagerness. "Pretend to be one of the girls' parents and offer him money in exchange for a visit."

"I like it." But she had serious doubts. "We don't know the names of any other members. I could try again at the soup kitchen to find out." Rox sipped her coffee. "But coming so soon after his outreach to the Carsons, he might be suspicious."

Marty looked a little deflated. "But a donation from somewhere—say, a church—might work."

"Maybe." But it still seemed too soon, too obvious. "Did you track down the owner of the land?"

Her stepdad nodded, perking up. "Charles Zumwalt lets the group live there nearly free. He considers it a charitable donation to a good cause. Plus, by keeping the utilities on and the landscaping maintained, he figures the occupants are actually helping the property retain its value."

Interesting concept. "Did you tell him what Blackstone is really like?"

"Zumwalt didn't want to hear it. He defended him and hung up."

Damn. "I'll bet the owner writes off the rent value as a donation somehow."

"So we'll report all of them to the IRS."

They drank their coffee in silence for a moment. Rox came back to the idea of shafting Blackstone while simultaneously extracting Emma. "What if we force all of them out? With a phony evacuation demand, for example? I'd like to disrupt the whole operation and rescue all of the girls if we can."

"I would too. But the scheme won't work if Blackstone tries to verify it."

She shrugged. "I know it's a long shot." What else would force someone to move? An eviction. "Here's a long-game idea. We make an offer to buy the land. Then Zumwalt has to give his tenants notice."

Marty let out a loud laugh. "We would have to have a letter of financing for Zumwalt to take the offer seriously. Unless you're hiding a pile of money, we'd be hard pressed to buy a cheap trailer right now."

Good point. They both had retirement accounts, but banks didn't consider those accessible income. They needed a rich proxy buyer. Rox snapped her fingers. "The Carsons have money. They can make the offer."

Marty cocked his head. "Then what? They don't really want to own twenty acres of rural land, do they?"

"We just need Zumwalt to give the charity an eviction notice. Force Blackstone to start hustling for a new place to live." Rox stood. *This could work.* "You and I can take turns watching the work camp. When Blackstone leaves to look at other properties, we make a move on Emma."

Marty shook his head. "I know I said I was all in, but we really don't want to do a straight-up kidnapping. We need to get Emma to come out willingly right after Blackstone leaves."

"I know. We will. But we need a good reason to access the property." Rox set her empty cup on the counter, eager to get going. "We have time to work on plan B while we get the real estate deal moving. First, I have to call the Carsons and get them on board."

Marty pushed out of his chair, moving slowly. "I'm going to grab a power nap while I wait for the caffeine to kick in."

She gave his shoulder a friendly punch. "Don't get old on me yet. I don't trust anyone else to do this work with me."

His eyes seemed to tighten. *Pain? Sadness?* "What is it?" she asked.

"Nothing." He popped her on the arm in return. "I just stayed up too late playing poker. Give me thirty minutes, and I'll be back on the job."

She watched him walk out and tried not to worry. He was only sixty-five. And pretty damn healthy except for the slightly high blood pressure. But most cops had that. A dark statistic crossed her mind. Many had short life-spans after putting down the badge. Rox shook it off. She reached for her work phone to call Jenny Carson, but her personal cell started ringing.

Her CIA buddy. "Hey, Sergio."

"Hey, MacFarlane."

No one had called her that since she'd left the CIA. When she'd been a cop, her fellow officers had called her Rocks to tease her about being hardheaded. "You find anything on Blackstone's military career?"

"Nothing serious. A few reprimands for fistfights. Both with another guy in his squad, Greg Loffland, who left the military around the same time. He was on that list I gave you earlier and lives in Portland. So Blackstone might still be in touch with him."

She hadn't realized Loffland was in the area. But he was another possible wedge, someone who might hold a grudge against Blackstone. She would have to sound Loffland out. "Do you have contact information?"

"Address and phone." Sergio rattled off the numbers, knowing she could process them quickly.

"Thank you. So how's the job? Is Kepart still snapping gum in your ear while he calls to report intel?" They both loved and hated working with the Istanbul-based agent.

A long pause. "He died of a heart attack two months ago."

No! Damn. "I'm sorry to hear that." Why hadn't anyone informed her? Because she'd been gone from the agency for more than a year, and it was a secretive organization. If Kepart's family hadn't known about his work, then agents couldn't exactly show up at his funeral service. They had to mourn privately. Rox didn't know what else to say. "I hope you'll stay in touch."

"Always." Sergio paused, and she could visualize him smiling. "I have to go."

"Thanks again." Rox hung up and keyed in the number he'd given her. The call went to voice mail. "This is Greg Loffland. Leave me a message."

A no-nonsense guy. She liked that. "This is Karina Jones. I'm an investigator, and I'd like to meet with you. This is about a military incident involving you and one of your squad mates. Please call me." That should get his attention. She hung up and contacted Jenny Carson.

Her client didn't answer but called right back instead. "Karina? Sorry, I was on the phone with my mother-in-law." Jenny sounded upset again. "I got the cash from her this morning, and she's not happy with me for actually letting Blackstone have it."

Oh hell. Did Dave Carson's money really belong to his mother? "Is the loss a problem?"

"It shouldn't be, but rich people can be stingy. Maybe that's why they're rich." Jenny seemed to get control of herself. "Sorry to be so emotional. My life was simpler before I married Dave. Sometimes I think this situation is my karma for stealing him from a friend." A long sigh. "And I wonder if Emma would be better off if she'd had a working-class childhood."

Again, Rox was flummoxed for how to respond. She stuck to the point of her call. "I have an idea for how to get her back. The scenario involves you and Dave making an offer on the land where Blackstone lives."

"How does that help?" A little annoyed now.

"An accepted offer would force the current owner to give the charity an eviction notice. That will rattle Blackstone and force him to leave the property, giving me an opportunity to confront and extract Emma."

"I don't know." Jenny's skepticism was thick. "Real estate transactions are slow, and the owner may negotiate to protect his tenants."

"They don't pay rent."

"That's even worse. Blackstone can go to court and demand a sixty-day notice."

Damn. That was news to her. "Talk it over with Dave and get back to me. I have another idea I'm working on too."

Jenny hesitated. "Can you help me get the ten thousand back?"

Seriously? "I really doubt that. Sorry." Rox hung up. Maybe it was time to resort to the phony inheritance scheme. It had worked with her last client. No, Blackstone was smart and suspicious. Rox had second thoughts about the ex-army buddy as well. He would probably be loyal to Blackstone, and meeting him in person could be a mistake. If he passed along her description to the cult leader, it might work against her, especially if this case ended up in court. She would wear a disguise when she met with him. Maybe the blonde wig this time, in case he was like Blackstone.

CHAPTER 15

Later that evening, Rox opened the fridge and realized she hadn't bought groceries in a while. Emma's case and the magnet treatments had occupied her thoughts. Maybe she should order pizza for her and Marty. He would love that, but his doctor wouldn't.

Her phone rang in the other room, and she hurried to pick it up. *Kyle.* Finally! "Hey, there."

"Hi." A pause. "Everything okay? You sound different."

"I'm just glad to hear from you."

"I'm sorry it took forever to call you back. But I've been working Bethany Grant's homicide nonstop."

"At least you were able to ID her."

"Blackstone gave us her name." Kyle lowered his voice. "I have time for a quick dinner if you want to join me."

Yes! "I'd love that." She would escape eating tuna salad and hopefully get some intel about Bethany's murder. "Sweet Basil in twenty minutes?"

"See you there." He hung up.

The abruptness bothered her. Would he always be that way? In the early stages, she'd been attracted to his direct, non-sentimental nature, but a little verbal affection would be nice.

◆ ◆ ◆

At the restaurant, she asked to be seated, knowing Kyle might be late. She picked up the menu just for fun and looked it over. Should she order something new? *Maybe.* She caught a waiter's attention and ordered an appetizer that looked interesting.

Kyle was late as expected, but she didn't mind. She'd worked as a police officer, so she accepted the unpredictable nature of his job. And damn he was good looking when he smiled. He apologized as he slid into the booth.

"You're fine." She glanced at the menu. "I ordered an appetizer called *pockets of love* just for the heck of it."

"Good. I'm starving. I missed lunch again."

"How's the case shaping up?"

"Completely confidential?"

"Always."

He leaned forward and said softly, "Blackstone has an alibi for the time of the murder, so we can't get a search warrant for his property. Also, the MO matches the I-5 Killer."

Blackstone probably wasn't the killer. Rox was both relieved and disappointed. "Did you get inside the work camp at all?"

"No." Kyle gave her a sympathetic look. "Sorry, but I didn't see Emma or even ask about her."

"It's okay. We know she's fine because she called her parents."

The waiter, a young man with horrible acne, brought the appetizer and coffee for Kyle. He'd waited on them a few times. "Ready to order?" He glanced at Rox. "The usual?"

"No, I think I'll try the beef stir-fry, the first one listed."

The waiter smiled. "Good choice."

Kyle raised an eyebrow. "Feeling adventurous, huh?" He turned to the waiter. "I'll have the house special."

When they had privacy again, Rox told Kyle about Emma's donation request and the meeting with her mother. "Blackstone took off the minute he got the money. Was any of that illegal?"

Kyle shook his head. "Not unless he fails to report the money on the charity's income statement."

Rox made a mental note to call the IRS about Sister Love. "What else did you learn about Blackstone? Or Bethany's murder? If you can share it."

Kyle lowered his voice again. "One of the members says Bethany was sneaking out to hook up with a neighborhood boy. We're still looking for him."

That surprised her. Bethany had sounded so pious at the soup kitchen. "That explains why she left the work camp. What's the theory? That the I-5 Killer picked her up while she was on her way to see the boyfriend?"

"Something like that. We'll see what the kid has to say." Kyle sipped his coffee. "When we find him. There aren't many houses out there, but a door-to-door canvass of the whole area would be ridiculously time consuming. We have to stay focused on identifying the serial killer."

Maybe she should find the boy herself. What if Bethany had told him secrets about the cult? Rox decided not to mention it to Kyle. "Any new leads on the killer from the recent crime scene?"

"Yes, but I can't tell you."

She felt better about holding back her own stuff. "I understand."

"How's your case coming along?"

"Slowly." She wanted to share more, but it seemed too risky for both of them.

"You seemed overly friendly a moment ago, and now you're holding back. What's going on?" When she didn't respond right away, Kyle asked, "How did your treatment go today?"

"I rescheduled for next week."

"Still feeling good about the results?"

"Mostly. Although I'm becoming aware that a lot of people aren't very happy."

He let out a small laugh. "You're lucky you waited until after your stint as a beat cop to get those treatments. The lowlifes would have been even harder to take."

She'd never thought of the people she encountered on the street as lowlifes. *Unfortunates* was her term for most of them.

Later, they stood near Rox's car, and she tried to decide if she should ask him to come over. They both had pending cases, and she didn't want him to feel pressured. She decided to wait until some of the workload was off. Still, she wanted to connect with him. Rox eased in and put her arms around his waist. "I've missed you."

Kyle gave her a quick squeeze and stepped away. "We're still in public."

"It's just a hug."

Under the ugly parking lot light, his brow furrowed. "Hugging didn't used to be important to you."

"It's not. I just needed some contact." She offered a silly grin to lighten the moment.

He let out an uncomfortable laugh. "I'm not sure I like the effect of the treatments."

She wasn't sure she did either, but she had expected his support. "Give it time." She started to say more, but her work phone rang in her purse, startling her. She slipped it out and looked at the ID. No name associated, but the number looked familiar.

"Anything related to Sister Love?" Kyle asked.

"I don't think so, but I'd better take it."

"Let's keep each other updated."

"Yes."

Kyle squeezed her shoulder and walked away. Rox felt disappointed, but the feeling faded as she answered the call. "Karina Jones. How can I help you?"

"This is Greg Loffland, returning your call. What is this about?" He had a thin, annoying voice.

"An incident between you and Deacon Blackstone. I'd like to meet. Are you still on Syracuse Street in northwest Portland?"

Her knowledge of his location made him hesitate for a long moment. "Why are you interested in something that happened years ago and was resolved by a military court?"

That sounded like a lot more than a fistfight. *Interesting.* She had to be careful. "We're investigating Blackstone and looking for leverage."

"How can I help?" His relief was palpable.

She tried to remember what she knew about his area. "Meet me at the Rose & Fiddle in an hour." It was a long drive, but hopefully worth it.

"How will I know who to look for?"

"Don't worry. I know what you look like." She hung up. Might as well keep him on edge.

Suddenly feeling anxious, she hurried to her car and drove home. In the house, she went straight to her bedroom and got the blonde wig she'd bought for her first extraction. Pulling it on eased some of her anxiety. She was no longer Rox MacFarlane, quirky analyst—she was Karina Jones, private investigator. But the meeting with Loffland still made her stomach clench. Saying things that were knowingly false was even harder than wearing something besides blue. Her atypical, compulsive brain wanted to override her effort. Should she put on the pink blouse Kyle had bought her? No, it was too dressy for the occasion. She added eyeliner and lipstick to her face, then grabbed a pair of nonprescription designer glasses to put on at the last minute. She hated wearing them even more than she hated jewelry. What else? She glanced in the mirror again. Too bad she couldn't disguise her height, but all she could do was make herself taller with heels, and that wouldn't help. Time to go.

◆ ◆ ◆

Without much traffic, the drive took less time than she thought, and Rox arrived at the tavern fifteen minutes early. She climbed out and looked around. The lot was full of trucks and older cars, and the brick building had never been power washed. A dive bar for sure. Maybe not a good choice. She'd picked the tavern because she'd heard of it when she was on patrol, but she had been inside only once, ten years earlier. Now she had second thoughts about meeting Loffland alone. What if he had called Blackstone, and the two of them planned to rough her up? The Glock was hidden in a secret compartment in her car, because she hated wearing it, even though she had a concealed-carry permit.

Rox climbed back in her car and called Marty. He would be unhappy that she'd done this without him, but as much as she loved working with him, his constant chatter could be annoying on a drive.

He answered immediately. "Hello." The TV blared in the background.

"Will you mute that?" The treatments obviously hadn't cured her noise sensitivity.

"Sure." The racket went silent. "What's going on?"

"I'm at the Rose & Fiddle, waiting to meet with Greg Loffland, a military friend of Blackstone's."

"What the hell? Why didn't you take me?"

Little white lies to her stepdad were easier. "I don't expect anything to come of it, and I didn't want to waste your time too." She launched into the meat of the situation before he could complain. "I just wanted you to know where I was and what I'm doing. If you don't hear from me in thirty minutes, call, okay?"

"Dammit, Rox. Now you've got me worried."

"Don't be. This is just a precaution. You know I can take care of myself." She had extensive self-defense training, but hadn't brushed up in years.

"Be careful."

"Talk to you soon." She hung up, climbed out again, and squared her shoulders. Looking confident was half the game.

Rox strode into the tavern, was immediately overwhelmed by the noise of the Friday-night crowd, and stepped back outside. She moved away from the door and leaned against the brick wall, hoping she didn't ruin her favorite spring jacket. She would wait, intercept Loffland when he arrived, and ask him to walk next door to the Mexican restaurant. That would throw off any plan he might have cooked up with Blackstone too.

Loffland showed up a few minutes later, his shaved dome gleaming in the blue neon light of the tavern's sign. She recognized his square face from the photo Sergio had sent with his file. But a vehicle hadn't pulled into the lot in the last few minutes, so he'd parked elsewhere and walked over. He was being cautious too. Rox stepped forward and called out his name.

He spun and came toward her. "Karina?"

"Yes. Walk with me." Rox turned toward the adjacent parking lot, but kept her eyes on Loffland.

He fell into step with her. "What alphabet federal branch are you with?"

"I can't tell you." They crossed into the next lot, and she noticed Loffland had a slight limp. Probably a war injury. "Thanks for meeting me." If he seemed cooperative, she would level with him about her real mission and ask for his help. Otherwise, this would be a short conversation.

Inside the restaurant, she slid into the booth near the door. Brightly painted in peach and aqua, the place was nearly empty. A short, stout waitress stopped by, and Rox ordered coffee she didn't plan to drink. Loffland asked for a tap beer.

When the server walked away, Rox asked, "How do you feel about Blackstone personally?"

Loffland's shoulders tightened. "We were good friends for a while when we served together. We've also had our differences. At the moment, he doesn't mean much to me."

A good sign. "Did you have a problem with him after you both left the army?"

"No, but I found out about something that happened while we were enlisted." Loffland shifted uncomfortably. "It's personal and nothing you can use."

She really wanted to know but wouldn't push him yet. "Do you know what Blackstone is involved in right now?"

"He runs a soup kitchen for veterans." Loffland rolled his eyes. "But that doesn't make him a good guy."

She sensed real animosity. "What else do you know about his charity?"

"Nothing. Why?" He leaned forward. "Is that what this is about? Is the charity a front for some scam?"

Time to risk the truth. "We think so. He recruits depressed and suicidal young girls. They work in the kitchen, as well as hit up motorists for donations."

"What the fuck?"

His outrage encouraged her. "He isolates them from their families too, then uses emotional blackmail to get the parents to donate to his cause."

"That's disgusting."

"There's a young woman I'm trying to extract from the group. Her parents haven't seen her in months. I could use your help." She had no intention of revealing Emma's name.

His eyes clouded a little. "You're not a federal investigator, are you?"

"I was. I'm private now." Rox had to keep him emotionally engaged. "Do you have any kids? A daughter?"

Loffland's mouth tightened. "No, but I plan to."

"I worry that Blackstone might be pressuring the girls for sex too."

A flash of anger in his eyes. "What do you need from me?"

"Just get Blackstone out of his complex for a few hours and let me know when the opening is."

"What—?" Loffland stopped, then asked, "When do you need this to happen?"

"As soon as possible."

"I'll see what I can set up." He shifted toward the outside of the booth. "Are we done here?"

"Do you need contact information for him?"

"Yeah, I guess so."

Didn't he already have it? "Try this." She wrote down the number Blackstone had used to contact Jenny Carson. "But it could be temporary. You may have to email through his website." Rox added that information to the napkin and passed it to him.

Loffland left without touching his beer. Rox pulled a ten out of her wallet, left it on the table, and followed him. In her car, she called Marty. "Hey, it went well. It looks like he's going to help us. Now, we just need a viable plan for getting Emma out."

CHAPTER 16

In the middle of a lengthy breakfast discussion with Marty, Rox realized she was going to have to make another trip to the work camp. "We need more intel. Such as, how many people are in the building during the day and where Emma will be when we arrive."

"We also need to know about their guns." Marty grimaced. "I'll be carrying, but I really don't want to shoot anyone."

Weapons were her biggest concern too. Ex-military people were likely to be armed, and rural Oregonians often were too. The combination put the statistical likelihood near 90 percent. "We won't let it go down like that. Still, I'd feel better if we could get Margo, the girlfriend, out of there. She could be trouble."

"With Blackstone gone, they might fall for a phony evacuation demand."

"We may not have time for that. The army buddy could call at the last minute, and we might have to move on the fly." Rox picked up their empty plates and tried to fit them into a full dishwasher. She really needed to get a few household chores done. She turned back to her step-dad. "I also want to find the neighbor boy that Bethany snuck out to see. He might know important details about the cult's day-to-day stuff."

"Didn't the task force already look for him?"

"I don't think so. Plus the kid is more likely to be home on a Saturday morning." What if they didn't locate him? How else could they find out what it was like inside the work camp? Besides knocking on the door. She snapped her fingers. "I could pretend to be a census taker and ask questions of whoever comes to the front."

Marty looked skeptical. "Maybe. But it's a risk to expose yourself to Blackstone." Her stepdad stood and downed the last of his coffee. "Let me do it. I can wear a nice jacket and look like a harmless old data collector."

She tried to visualize the scene and almost laughed. Then she remembered their last trip out there. "The dog could be a problem."

"Crap. I'd forgotten about it."

"It looked wild, so it may not be connected to Blackstone. Or it belongs to the house we parked by." Rox stood, eager to get going. "We'll take reading glasses and clipboards and canvass the area. Maybe the neighbors will provide information." She smiled. "I'll even put on a skirt."

"You own a skirt?" Marty laughed.

"Bite me." Rox gestured for him to get moving. "You still have clipboards, right? You used to give them to us when we went on long drives. Jo would draw, and I would create and solve math problems."

"You did some writing too." He walked toward the front door.

"I remember." Rox headed for her bedroom. She would take pants as well, in case she needed to change.

The morning fog cleared as they drove south, and by the time they turned on Barton Road, the sky was a glorious blue. Still her favorite color. She hoped the weather would hold for the actual mission. Buckets of rain could be a problem. Or maybe not. An idea percolated in her brain.

She turned to Marty, who was driving. "For the extraction, I could pretend to have car trouble or be lost and need to borrow a cell phone."

"That doesn't get you inside."

"Needing to use the restroom might. Or I could fake an injury. Women are sympathetic to such things."

"Blackstone's girlfriend might not be. You have to be pretty cold to exploit vulnerable young women." Marty slowed as the first rural home came into view.

"Let's not stop here. We need to start with the house closest to the work camp."

"That makes sense." He pressed the accelerator, and the big sedan lurched forward. They'd taken his car because it looked more *government* than her Cube or the truck.

A few minutes later, they pulled into the driveway on the corner of the turnoff road. Old and small but well maintained, the cottage had a Disney look with climbing vines and red shutters.

"Does Snow White live here?" Marty chortled.

"I was wondering the same thing." Rox glanced around the property. A chicken coop in the side yard, but no dog. "Ready? I'll take the lead."

"I've got more experience." Marty gave her a look as they climbed out.

"Females are less intimidating."

As they walked up the stone path, an older woman opened the front door. "I'm not buying anything!" She started to step back inside.

"Wait! We're not selling." Rox quickened her pace. "We're collecting census information." It was a crime to impersonate a federal employee, but she hadn't claimed to be with the government, so it shouldn't matter.

"There's not much to tell. I'm the only one here." The old woman's voice broke on the last word.

Was everyone unhappy? Rox ignored the emotions and plunged right in. "Can you tell us anything about the occupants of the place down the road?" She pointed in the direction of the concrete buildings. "We're having trouble getting information from them."

"Not really." Her brow creased. "They moved in about two years ago, and it seems to be a bunch of teenage girls."

"Do you know how many?" Rox glanced at her clipboard for effect.

"Not for sure. But I see a group leave in the van in the morning and a different bunch go out at night. At least, I think they're different girls. A man lives there too, but I've only seen him a few times." She shook her head and made a tsking sound. "It's not right, him living there with all those girls."

None of this was new information. "Is that it? Just the man and what, ten or fifteen girls?"

"An older woman too. Well, not old, but middle-aged. She leaves nearly every night too, wearing the same hospital scrubs as the girls."

So Margo worked the night shift as a caregiver still. Good to know. "What time does she leave?"

"Around eight, I think." The old woman squinted. "Why does the census need to know that?"

Good question.

Marty chimed in. "We collect employment data too. Do you have a job?"

"Good grief, no. I'm nearly eighty."

Rox decided they should wrap it up before the woman got suspicious. "Are there any other teenagers in the area? Young boys or just the girls?"

She scowled again. "There's a family down the road, near the dairy. I see boys in the yard sometimes when I go into town to shop. They're usually jumping on that foolish trampoline."

"What age?"

"Teenagers, like you said."

Yes! They may have found Bethany's boyfriend. Rox jotted something on the blank paper on her clipboard. "Thanks for your time."

"Seems like a waste of government money to me." The old woman shut the door.

On the way down the path, Marty muttered out of the side of his mouth, "You forgot to ask her name."

Rox laughed. "She didn't seem to notice."

They climbed into the sedan, and Marty turned to her. "Where now?"

"A quick trip by the work camp, then the house by the dairy. I think we might find the guy Bethany was sneaking out to see."

"You want to actually pass in front of the property on a dead-end lane?" Marty asked. "Remember, this car looks like something a federal agent would drive." He pulled out and turned down the narrow asphalt road.

"Good point. Let's just find a place nearby where we can do recon and surveillance."

As they drove slowly forward, Rox scanned the area. Fir and oak trees lined the road, with a few patches of clear-cut that had driveway turnoffs going nowhere. The county had probably planned for housing that never developed. About a hundred yards before the concrete buildings came into full view on the left, they spotted another turnoff. This one led into the forest. "There. Turn down that logging road."

Marty made a sudden left, and they bounced down the dirt lane. After fifty yards, he turned the big car around and parked next to a wide-based tree. "I think we're out of sight here."

"Do you have binoculars?" She was already looking in his glovebox. "Yep." She held them to her eyes and scanned through the trees. "I have a filtered view of the work camp from here. Three cars today. The Bronco, the minivan, and a smaller car. I don't recognize the make."

"Anything going on?"

She shifted her gaze. "That might be Emma in the garden. If so, that's good. We know she's not locked up when she's here." Rox hadn't been as worried about that since Emma had met with her mother.

"Should we go?" Marty asked. "You said Loffland could call at a moment's notice, so let's find the neighbor boy while we can."

"Roger that."

Ten minutes later, they spotted a mobile home, then beyond it down the road, a small dairy. No vehicles were in the yard, so Marty pulled in. The run-down trailer was as different from the fairy-tale cottage as possible. Paint peeling, gutters hanging loose, and junk lying everywhere. The trampoline was in a side yard on a small patch of weeds, surrounded by piles of firewood and rusty vehicles.

"This place gives me a bad vibe," Rox announced.

"Me too." Marty shut off the engine, but didn't reach for the door handle. "They probably have guns and don't like visitors, especially from the *guv'ment*."

Nobody in Oregon pronounced it like that, but he was making a point. Rox tried to make the case for proceeding. "We need to ask the kid if he saw Bethany that night." She wasn't yet convinced that Blackstone was innocent of the girl's murder.

"Yep. And we need to see if he knows about the inner workings of the cult."

Neither of them moved.

"It doesn't look like anyone who drives is home," Rox noted. "They're no working cars here."

"Let's do this." Marty climbed out, not carrying his clipboard.

She followed him toward the door, her hands free too. "If the census taker idea doesn't seem workable, we'll switch it up and say we're private investigators looking into Bethany's murder."

"We're about to get the door slammed in our face either way." Marty talked through clenched teeth, and Rox realized he was more nervous than she was. But he'd been a cop a lot longer.

As they neared the small porch, barking started inside the house.

Marty swore under his breath, a rare display of vulgarity. Rox knocked on the door, her gut clenched.

A blond boy, around fourteen, opened the door. "Who are you?" Slender and freckled, he looked quite innocent.

"We're private investigators," Rox said. "We're looking for information about a girl named Bethany. She lived in the concrete work camp not far from here."

The boy blinked rapidly. "You said *lived*. Did she move away?"

The dog was still barking but not as loudly, and it hadn't shown up at the door. Rox felt Marty relax a little. "Not exactly. Did you know her?"

"No, but my brother does." He turned and yelled, "Noah! Get out here."

A moment later, another teenager appeared, taller and older, but nearly identical to the first boy. "What's up?"

"I'm sorry, but Bethany's dead, and we're investigating her murder." Rox softened her voice to almost a plea. "Can we come in?"

The younger boy shook his head. "We're not allowed."

Noah swallowed hard, and panic flashed across his face. "Murdered? When?"

Apparently he hadn't heard or watched the news. "Wednesday night. Did you see her that evening?"

"Why? You think I killed her? That's fucked up."

Marty kept quiet, so Rox pressed forward, trying to find the balance between showing empathy and getting results. Not her strong suit. "We know she was your friend and this is hard for you, but we need to find out what happened."

His eyes went wide, and he blinked rapidly like his brother had done. "Are the police looking for me?"

"Probably. But you're not a prime suspect. Just tell me if you saw her Wednesday night."

"I don't know. And I shouldn't be talking to you." He started to close the door.

"Wait!" Marty reached to catch it. "If you talk to us and cooperate, the police will go easy on you. Otherwise, they might take you in for questioning. You won't like that."

For a long moment, Noah hesitated.

The younger boy elbowed him. "Just tell them the truth."

Rox waited him out.

Finally Noah said, "I did see Bethany Wednesday night for about an hour. She could never stay long."

Kyle would definitely want to question this young man. "When did she leave here?"

"I'm not sure. After dark though."

The sun had set around eight the night before. "Did she talk about her life in the cult?"

"What do you mean? I thought Sister Love was a charity."

Rox backtracked. "It is a charity, but some of the members' parents are worried."

Noah's face tightened. "Bethany's parents are dead. Her mom died when she was little, and she killed her father accidentally."

Poor girl! No wonder she had grief and self-esteem issues. But it was time to get specifics. "Do you know how many girls live there?"

"Twelve or so, I think."

"Are most of them home during the day?"

He shrugged. "Bethany worked in the soup kitchen, but other girls went into the city to ask for money."

So only the cult leaders and the truck stop crew were home during the day. Six or seven people. "Did Bethany ever talk about Margo?"

"Not really."

"Did she ever mention a girl named Emma?"

"Yeah, she liked Emma." Noah suddenly squinted. "Why?"

Marty chimed in. "We're trying to establish who had motive to kill her."

The kid's lips trembled. "I don't know why anyone would. Bethany was the nicest girl I've ever known, but she thought she needed to be punished."

A shiver of worry ran through Rox. "What do you mean? Was she mistreated at the work camp?"

"Sometimes, but she thought she'd earned it."

An old rage simmered. Jolene had been abused too, not just sexually but physically.

An engine rumbled behind them, and Rox glanced over her shoulder. A pickup truck pulled into the driveway. *Dad was home.* She glanced at Marty. He'd turned to face the newcomer, shoulders stiff, one hand at his waist, ready to reach for his weapon.

"You'd better go." Noah slammed the door.

The man in the truck grabbed a shotgun from the rack behind him, jumped out, and rushed toward them. "What are you doing here talking to my boys?" He was blond and freckled like his sons, but had lost his innocent look long ago.

Heart rate ticking up, Rox stepped off the small porch and headed for the car. "His girlfriend was murdered, and we had some questions. You can expect a visit from the police too." She hoped a bigger worry would distract him.

He stopped and stared, showing a brief uncertainty. Then the man raised his shotgun. "Get the hell off my property!"

They complied.

CHAPTER 17

After Marty finally left to play golf that afternoon, Rox picked up her phone. She'd been putting off calling Kyle, but it was time. The longer she waited, the more upset he would be. Or maybe he wouldn't mind that much. They'd never had overlapping investigations before, so this was a unique situation. She had every right to pursue her own leads. But still, the neighborhood boyfriend information had come from him. And Kyle had seemed uncomfortable with her the last time they'd met up.

She pressed the icon to his number, sucked in a deep breath, and hoped for his message service. But he answered this time. "Hey, Rox. This has to be brief. I have a team meeting in a few minutes."

"Got it. I found the neighborhood boy Bethany was seeing. His name is Noah Carpenter." She'd checked their mailbox on the way out earlier. Marty's idea. Her impulse had been to get the hell away before the shotgun dude put holes in the back of the car. Or her head.

Kyle was silent, so she added, "The kid saw Bethany Wednesday night sometime between seven and eight thirty."

"Thanks for the information, but how am I going to explain to the team that you even knew to look for him?"

She'd given the logistics some thought. "Bethany told me she had a neighborhood boyfriend when I talked to her at the soup kitchen. I decided to find him to get information about my case."

She'd never lied to Kyle before, and it didn't bother her as much as it should have. But Kyle knew she was fabricating the detail to protect him. He would understand. Wouldn't he? Were the treatments making her more deceptive?

A long pause. "You should have let the task force handle it. The boy could be spooked now and refuse to talk to us."

Yeah, but that may have been the case either way. "Sorry. I needed intel about the cult, and the members aren't exactly available and open."

Another hesitation. "What else did you learn?"

Now he wanted the scoop, of course. "Blackstone physically abuses the girls."

"I'm not surprised. But we need one of them to file charges before we can do anything. I have to go. Call you later." Kyle hung up.

Was he mad? He'd been distant and abrupt with her lately. Rox pushed the thought out of her head, sat down, and relaxed for the first time that day. So much still needed to be done—especially in her quest to shut down Sister Love—but she needed a moment to chill and let the tension out of her body. She leaned back in her recliner and closed her eyes.

She woke to the sound of her burner cell. What time was it? Had she fallen asleep? Rox grabbed her phone and looked at the caller's ID. No name, just the familiar number. Greg Loffland. *Damn!* She'd meant to call him earlier and request that he set up the scenario with Blackstone some evening. Too late for that. "Karina Jones."

"Greg Loffland. I'm meeting Deacon tomorrow at two o'clock. We're having a beer at the Henry's on Twelfth Street."

A centrally located tavern in downtown Portland. Not that it mattered, except for how long Blackstone would be out. "Any chance of pushing that back until tomorrow night, say around eight?" If possible, she wanted Margo to be gone from the complex as well.

"I'll try. But if you don't hear from me, you'll be clear to go at two."

"Thanks. You're doing the right thing for a lot of young women and their families."

"Good luck." The call clicked off.

Tension tugged at her shoulders again. This could be her most dangerous extraction yet. Her first had required her to grab a ten-year-old boy away from his abusive father. It had been risky because her window of opportunity was brief, but distracting the father had been simple. He wasn't very bright, just mean and controlling.

Breaching the work camp would be challenging, especially with Blackstone's girlfriend at home. Could they get Margo out? Pulling off a motorist-in-need ruse would be easier with only the young members at home. Anyone in a cult had to be vulnerable to suggestion and authority, and these girls believed in a life of service, so they would likely help her. But how to get Margo out? A fake call from work to come in early? They didn't know where she worked yet, and even if they found out, she could say no. A phony call from a family member? Or someone wanting to make a donation? Money was always a good motivator. But they didn't even have Margo's phone number. *Damn.* They weren't ready yet.

A wild idea played out in her head. She could carry chloroform and incapacitate Margo if she interfered. Hell, she could drug Emma too and just carry her out. Rox shuddered. Only if the girl's life were in imminent danger. And it didn't seem to be. Rox needed more information about Margo. She'd already searched online and found nothing except an arrest ten years earlier for a DUI. No social media at all. Blackstone probably didn't allow it. That left three sources: Margo's employer, the girls at the truck stop, and the girls at the soup kitchen. The kitchen seemed like the most direct. Should she rent the nun's habit again or try something new?

Too impatient to drive over to the party shop, she opted for posing as a reporter looking for interesting women to interview. Still wearing the damn skirt from earlier, she already looked the part. Somewhat. Rox pulled on the blonde wig again and scooped it into a bun, then added a conservative pair of reading glasses. Reporters carried digital recorders, and she had one in the second drawer of her desk. She found it right where it was supposed to be. Disguises and pretexts still made her nervous, but she was getting better at it. The bureau had probably been right to keep her out of the field. Direct and compulsive, her natural mode, didn't go well with spying and subtlety. She resorted to it only to help young people who needed to be rescued from oppressive or abusive situations. She owed it to Jolene.

Rox checked herself in the mirror and frowned. The getup looked more librarian than reporter, but it probably didn't matter. As long as she could coax one of the Sister Love members to talk—but not be able to identify her if this case ended up in court. Rox hurried out, feeling guilty again for not taking Marty. But she didn't need him for this, and they already spent way too much time together. Sometimes she worried that it was unhealthy. Thank goodness he was dating someone now. She would have to ask him about the woman after they completed the extraction; Marty was like her and would want to bring up the relationship at his own timing.

On the drive over, she called him, hoping he was still out golfing and wouldn't answer. She got lucky and left him a message with an update that the extraction was happening tomorrow afternoon.

When she walked into the soup kitchen, a wave of uncertainty hit her. The nun's habit she'd worn the first time had made her feel obscure and safe, but now she felt exposed. Bethany's murder might have made the other members wary. This effort could not only be a waste of time, it could backfire and make Blackstone and the girls close ranks. But her body kept moving forward, even though her brain wanted to retreat. Rox passed the tables where only a few homeless men were seated and walked up to the serving counter.

The mid-twenties member who'd interrupted her last time turned to stare at her. "We only serve the indigent."

What was her name? Bethany had mentioned it briefly. Rox smiled. "I'm Karina Jones, a freelance writer. Have you got a few minutes to talk?"

"About what?" The woman tipped her head, suspicion making her face look even more weathered. This member had either been an addict or homeless or both, and her yellow scrubs didn't make her look any more trustworthy. Considering a lot of jails made their inmates wear scrubs, the uniform had lost its social value.

"I write about interesting women who are doing good work," Rox said. "What's your name?"

"Ronnie. But I'm not going to tell you anything about Sister Love. We don't take any recognition for the work we do." She twisted the white towel she was gripping.

"I understand, Ronnie, but I'd like to talk to your founder, Margo Preston. I want to know what motivated her to help create Sister Love."

Ronnie's eyes softened. "My mother never gets credit for her part in this charity, but I don't think she'll want to be interviewed."

Her mother! That information was gold. Now Rox knew Margo's weakness, possibly, and might be able to use it to get her out of the complex. "I'd like to ask Ms. Preston anyway. Can you give me her contact information?"

Ronnie shook her head. "I'd better not."

"What if this is your mom's only opportunity to tell her story? You don't want her to miss that." Rox remembered to smile. "I promise to call her once and throw the number away." That was sort of true. But once she had a phone number in her head, it belonged to her.

Ronnie worked her mouth around while she thought it over. "I suppose. Ready?"

Oh, she needed to pretend to write it down or put it in her phone—even though the number would stay in her brain without either effort. Rox pulled out her burner cell, even though she didn't plan to call

Margo from it. "Ready. I'll delete the contact after I've talked with your mother."

Ronnie glanced at the other Sister Love girls, who were busy with chores, then said the number quickly and quietly. Rox keyed it in. Another gold strike! She was tempted to take her intel and leave, but what if she could learn more? She looked up at Ronnie. "What's your motivation for doing this work? To help your mom, or is it personal?"

The woman shrugged. "It's better than the life I had before. I'd better get back to work." She turned away.

"What if sharing your story could help other young girls?" Rox called after her.

The other members in blue scrubs turned at her raised voice. Ronnie gestured for Rox to leave, and she decided not to push her luck. She started to say thanks, then realized it might get Ronnie in trouble with Blackstone if the other girls thought Ronnie had talked to a reporter. As Rox walked out, she marveled at the insight. Making that connection would have never happened before her treatment. She liked her new and improved brain and vowed to not skip any more appointments.

On the drive home, she worked through several scenarios for getting Margo to leave the camp. They all involved an emergency with her daughter. Rox's favorite was to make a call from a hospital ER, saying Ronnie had been in an accident. Yes, it was mean and would give Margo a few minutes of worry. But what Margo was doing to the Sister Love members—or at least turning a blind eye to—was revolting. Now that Rox suspected the girls were being physically abused, she wanted Blackstone to go to prison. And the abuse probably went deeper. Cult leaders were notorious for sexually exploiting the young women in their following. And if Margo knew about the abuse, maybe she would get convicted too. The whole case could take the police months to investigate. In the meantime, she had to get Emma out and earn her fee.

As she neared the duplex, Rox called Marty. "Hey, pal. I've got good news."

"About time. What's the word?"

"Ronnie, the older member I told you about, is Margo Preston's daughter. We can exploit that to get Margo out of the complex right after Blackstone leaves."

"I'll sleep better tonight knowing that."

"Me too. And I have Margo's phone number."

"How the hell did you get all that?"

"Another trip to the soup kitchen, posing as a freelance writer." Rox was proud of her performance. "Pretending that I admired Margo enough to want to interview her was challenging."

"Could you have done it before your treatment?"

"Maybe, but I would have been less believable."

"Are you gonna start wearing something besides blue?"

The blue bothered him? He mostly wore blue, gray, and white. Marty laughed, and she relaxed. "Maybe some teal or violet," she joked. "Blue has been good to me, so I can't abandon it."

"As a former cop, me neither."

At home, she heated up a frozen pizza and sat down to watch the news. After a few minutes of watching another bomb report, she shut off the TV. Shaking, she had to sit for a minute before she could eat dinner. Working at the CIA and learning just how devious and evil terrorist organizations were had made her hypersensitive to the subject. Mass shootings were becoming like that for her too. She wanted to be informed, but all the death was overwhelming.

After she washed up, she headed to her desk and took out her case file. A piece of this operation was still missing, something she'd forgotten to do. She suddenly realized what it was and called her client. Jenny Carson didn't answer, so Rox left a message: "I'm attempting an extraction tomorrow afternoon. Have the deprogramming specialist ready to step in." She hoped the Carsons had found someone as she'd suggested.

Rox hung up and read through her notes, hoping to find a loose end, a piece of research she could do this evening to be productive. Halfway through, her burner phone rang. Not Jenny or Greg Loffland. Another client? That would be surprising. With some reluctance, she answered. "Hello?"

"Is this Karina Jones?"

She didn't recognize the voice, and he sounded a little drunk or high. "Yes. Who is this?"

"Just think of me as the guy you fucked over when you took my son. The state has him now, and when I find you, you're gonna pay." He hung up.

CHAPTER 18

Detective Kyle Wilson parked in the lot behind the Sister Love soup kitchen and climbed from his unmarked sedan. The area was overrun with homeless people and a bit sketchy. But that didn't stop fifty people from standing in line at the Voodoo Doughnut shop across the street on a Sunday morning. He rounded the building and saw a line at the charity kitchen too. Blackstone's work crew wouldn't appreciate having to stop and answer questions right now, but murder investigations didn't run according to witness convenience.

The ragged men ignored his polite attempts to bypass the line, so Wilson called out, "Police, let me through."

They grudgingly parted, and he stepped into the dark, ugly building that was filled with a delicious simmering smell. He pushed his way to the counter and tried to get the attention of the first woman on the line. Her yellow scrubs and meth-scarred face surprised him. Another detective had been here a few days before, but he hadn't reported what the crew was wearing, and Rox had indicated the girls were all young. Probably none of it mattered. This was likely a dead end for the murder case, but he was still trying to find Bethany's family. The rest of his team was more focused on finding the serial killer. But they needed to notify Bethany's next of kin, and he was behind on the task. The whole department had been sidetracked for two days with a shooting at a library, and they were just now getting back to their regular duties.

When the woman finally looked at him, he said, "Detective Wilson, Portland PD. I need to ask a few questions about Bethany Grant."

The woman grimaced. Grief or frustration, he couldn't tell. "Can it wait a few hours? We're kinda busy here." A little sarcasm.

"I see that, and I won't take up much of your time. Can we step out back where it's quiet?"

"I'll give you five minutes." The woman turned to the other girls, who were much younger. "I'm stepping out for a cigarette break."

The closest one, wearing blue scrubs, rolled her eyes but didn't respond.

Wilson walked around the end of the counter and followed the woman in yellow out the back door. She lit a smoke, took a deep drag, and leaned against the back wall.

"What's your name?"

"Ronnie." She eyeballed him. "You find Bethany's killer yet?"

Her attitude annoyed him. "I'll ask the questions."

"Whatever."

"What do you know about Bethany's life outside the charity?"

"Not much. We leave our past behind."

Yeah, right. "Where was she from?" They hadn't found the victim in the DMV database, nor did she have an Oregon birth certificate.

"Northern Cali, somewhere. Some coastal town that started with an *i* or an *e.*"

That narrowed it down a little. "Eureka?"

"Maybe. We didn't talk much."

"Who did talk to her?"

"Don't know." The heavy woman gave a small shrug.

"Do you know anything else about Bethany?"

"Not really."

This was a dead end. But just in case Bethany's murder had been personal but made to look like the work of the serial killer, he tried a more traditional approach. "Was there anyone new in her life? Someone unexpected?"

Ronnie took another drag and said, "A nun came in and chatted with Bethany a few days ago. That was kind of odd."

A wave of discomfort hit him. "What day and what time?"

"Last week. Maybe Wednesday afternoon. That's the best I can remember."

The day Rox had been here. "What did they talk about?"

"Bethany said the nun wanted to recruit her."

"What did the nun look like?"

Ronnie rolled her eyes. "Ugly black dress. You know."

"What size person? Tall, short, fat? Give me something."

"Tall, but not fat. Sort of pretty."

It could have been Rox. *Damn.* Why hadn't she told him? And what else was she keeping from him about this case? He really cared about her, but she could be so stubborn. Plus, the treatments were changing her personality, and he didn't know what to expect from her anymore. "Thanks for your time." He handed Ronnie a business card. "If you think of anything else you know about Bethany, please call me. I need to find her family."

Already in the back lot, Wilson turned and walked toward his car. This was the weirdest case. The victim had no ID, no cell phone, no computer, and no personal effects to search. And they still had no idea who she really was.

Abruptly Ronnie called after him, "Bethany killed her father, so I don't think she has any family to find."

Wilson spun back. "What do you mean?"

"She accidentally shot her father when they were doing target practice, and I think he was the only family she had."

Bizarre! But it also explained why she'd joined the guilt cult. Now the poor girl had been murdered, mostly likely by a psychopath. "Do you know the father's name?"

"No." Ronnie flicked her cigarette down and went back inside.

As Wilson drove back to the department, he considered calling Rox, then decided to wait. He would rather confront her in person and look in her eyes when they talked. The magnet treatments had changed her, and she seemed less direct and more emotional now. He cared about her, but it wasn't a good combination for him. He wanted more affection from her, but not in public. And he needed her to be consistent. His job made most of his life chaotic, and he needed his girlfriend and potential life partner to be predictable. With her blue shirts and direct, deadpan responses, Rox had been that. But now he didn't even know if he trusted her to always level with him.

At his desk, he got online, found the Eureka Police Department, and made the call. After identifying himself and the nature of his inquiry, he was finally connected to Detective Allen Walsh. "I need to know about Bethany Grant. She was murdered here in Portland, Oregon, and I'm looking for her family."

"Wow. That's damn sad." Papers rustled in the background. "The girl accidentally shot her father a year or so ago, then tried to commit suicide." He paused, as if trying to recall. "She was in a treatment center for a while, then disappeared after she was released."

Walsh was a slow talker, and Wilson made notes as he listened. The backstory was interesting, but not what he needed to know. "What about her other family? I need to notify someone so they can claim her body."

"There's no one that I know of. The dad was an only child, and so was Bethany." The other detective made a mulling-over throat sound. "I wonder what happens to the royalties now."

"What royalties?"

"Barrett Grant was a writer. Science fiction, I think. He had a monthly income from his books that he left to Bethany in a trust."

Also interesting. "How much money?"

"I'm trying to remember. But I think it was several thousand a month."

The Eureka PD had probably seen the financials at the time of the father's death. "Do you still have a copy of the will?"

"I don't know. I'll check."

"Fax it to me, please. Along with whatever financial and banking information you have." Wilson rattled off his fax number, hoping he didn't have to make a trip to California. "Did you ever suspect the daughter of murder?"

"Of course." The slow drawl was gone. "But that girl was so distraught, we quickly let go of the idea. Besides, Grant didn't have much in the bank at the time, just the latest royalty payment."

"Anything else I should know?"

"Nope. I hope you catch her killer. Good luck." Walsh ended the call.

Wilson silently cursed the new information. Not only was there no one to claim the body, but now that money was a possible motive, the task force had to reconsider Blackstone—and everyone in the cult—as suspects. First, he needed a look at Barrett Grant's will and finances. Maybe it wasn't enough money to kill for. Had Bethany left a will? Doubtful. If she hadn't, where would the royalties go? Did they come by check, or were they directly deposited? *Shit.* This was getting complicated, and he had just wanted to send the poor girl home.

CHAPTER 19

Sunday, April 23, 8:35 a.m.

After a morning dance session and shower, Rox headed over to Marty's for their traditional Sunday breakfast. He liked to make French toast and bacon, and she was happy to eat it. Thank god her size and healthy metabolism burned off almost everything. She knocked, he called out, "Clear," and she stepped into his side of the duplex. She glanced around for signs that his new girlfriend had stayed over but didn't see any. The side-by-side recliners didn't have any pillows or blankets added, and she didn't smell any perfume. The wall filled with sports photos and memorabilia still visually bothered her, so clearly parts of her brain hadn't been affected by the treatment. The blanket made of MacFarlane tartan still hung over the couch. She hated the damn thing. But she kind of loved it too, despite its garish red-and-black plaid.

"Good morning," Marty called cheerfully from the kitchen.

Maybe he had gotten laid the night before while she was working. Good for him. "Morning." Rox walked into the kitchen, and the smell of crispy bacon overwhelmed her. She snagged a piece from the plate where it cooled and munched it. "You ready to tell me about your girlfriend?"

"Not yet." He grinned and transferred food from the counter to the table. "Let's eat and plan this mission."

◆ ◆ ◆

After they'd cleared the dishes, Rox finally told him about the threatening phone call the night before.

"Son of a bitch!" Marty slammed down his empty coffee cup. "Do you know who it was?"

It was more reaction than she'd expected. "My best guess is Marcus Cubano, the guy we took the little boy away from in our first case." She'd had only four extractions in the year and a half she'd been a private investigator. "His wife was our client. And if the state has custody of the kid now, then she messed up."

"How did he get your Karina Jones number?"

"Good question. She probably went back to the prick and told him."

Marty shook his head, obviously disgusted. "I don't understand why women stay with abusive men."

Jolene was the unspoken mystery, as always. They would never really know how a smart, confident woman had ended up in an abusive multiple marriage. But Rox knew the scenarios were always more complicated than they seemed on the surface. And this subject was always personal for both of them. "Don't think about Jo," she pleaded. "Or my safety. It's probably an empty threat. He sounded a little drunk."

"What if Cubano finds you?" Marty stood, his body stiff with tension.

"I've covered my tracks well."

"We have to find him first."

She shook her head. "No, let's stay focused on getting Emma out. Then we'll worry about Cubano." Rox stood, feeling too worked up to sit any longer. "And we still have to shut down the charity."

"Blackstone needs prison time," Marty snarled. "I can't believe he's physically abusing those poor girls who already feel so bad about themselves."

Her stepdad was such a good man. Maybe that was the reason she'd never dated anyone for more than a year. Most men just didn't measure up to his level. Kyle might though. She shook off the thought. "Let's run through the plan again, then head out. I'd rather sit in a stakeout at the complex than wait it out here."

"I'm with you on that." Marty suddenly grabbed both her arms, like he had when she was a child and he needed her undivided attention. "Promise me you won't go anywhere by yourself until we resolve the Cubano issue."

She wondered what he had in mind. "What's your plan? Break his leg?"

A wicked smile distorted his sweet face. "That would slow him down and keep him from coming after you."

"Or it might make him even more determined. We might have to put him in jail too."

"I have an idea for that, but I'm not going to share it yet." Marty nodded. "To protect you from knowing."

"Let's focus." She snapped her fingers. "I'll watch the work camp and let you know when Blackstone leaves. Then you make the call from the Riverview Medical Clinic." It was the urgent care facility halfway between the soup kitchen and the compound. "When Margo takes off, I'll notify you and you haul ass over to where I'm waiting." She was glad they'd found the nearby spot in advance. She'd also checked to make sure Ronnie was at work.

Marty chimed in with the rest of the plan. "You drive up to the complex and ask to use a phone and the restroom. Once inside, you text me that it's a go."

Rox nodded. This was the part of the scenario that could go five different ways. "I find Emma, say her mother's having an emergency, and drag her out if I have to. You're waiting outside, on foot, to watch for trouble and assist if needed." They wanted only one vehicle to deal with at that point—in case Emma tried to resist or bolt.

Marty grinned. "Then I drive like a bat out of hell away from the work camp, while you talk to the girl and help her realize Blackstone is a predator."

"I'll tell her she can live a life of service through the Peace Corps or Habitat for Humanity just to lure her out," Rox added. "Don't forget to call Mrs. Carson and let her know we're coming." Jenny Carson had called back the night before and was scrambling to find a deprogramming specialist who could work with them right away and help the girl process her guilt.

"I think we're about ready." Marty nodded at her.

Full panic suddenly set in, and Rox had to take deep breaths. Would she ever be an old pro at this? As a cop, she'd had a badge and gun to back up her bold moves and protect her legally. This could turn into a kidnapping. She could go to prison.

"You okay?"

"I will be." Rox straightened her shoulders and started forward. "Why are you so calm about this? You know we could get rolled up for years."

"Emma won't file charges. Girls with low self-esteem never do. Besides, at this point, I don't have much to lose." He tipped his Blazers cap and stepped outside.

Rox followed him. "What the hell does that mean?"

"Nothing, sweetie." A sadness in his eyes. "But we both know cops don't live long lives. And golfing bores me. Without these cases, I'd eat my gun."

She didn't believe that. As Marty locked his door, she said, "I thought you were dating."

"I am, but we're just friends, having fun."

He'd had lots of girlfriends over the years, but they'd never gotten serious or moved in. When they were young, she and Jo had been the focus of his life, and he hadn't let go of that yet. "Maybe it's time you got serious about somebody."

"Right after you do." Marty laughed, then looked her over. "You going like that?"

Rox glanced at her clothes, jeans and a light-blue T-shirt. "What's wrong?"

"They can ID you."

"Oh shit." She'd been so preoccupied with the plan itself, she'd forgotten her disguise. "Give me five minutes."

Rox hurried next door to her place. She had a curly red wig she'd worn once and wanted to try again. Some sunglasses this time too. Maybe some pale foundation.

When she returned to Marty's, he had a serious look on his face as he handed her a small black pouch.

Rox was afraid to open it.

"Chloroform and a rag. Just in case things go south."

Both relieved and a little freaked out, Rox slipped the pouch into her shoulder bag. She rarely took a purse with her anywhere, but today it matched the part she was playing.

"Let's do this."

On the drive south to the work camp, Rox ran through half a dozen scenarios in her head. In most, Emma refused to come along, and Rox had to manhandle her, maybe use the chloroform. She kept seeing the other members coming to help their sister and herself taking a lot of blows from frightened young women. Even in her mind, in self-defense, she couldn't bring herself to strike any of the girls. Rox almost contacted Marty twice to call it off. But dammit, they had to try. She just had to be very convincing. She'd never done any acting—except for small bits during the brief extractions she'd conducted. *And the nun routine,* she reminded herself. She'd been developing her field agent and operative skills for more than a year, and now her brain was functioning in new ways. She could do this! The hardest part would be after Emma realized there was no emergency. She would have only a brief opportunity to quickly and effectively persuade the girl she could find peace of mind in a better way. She would use her own personal experience of Jolene's murder at the hands of a cult leader if she had to.

Deep into practicing what she would say, Rox missed the turn onto the unmarked road and had to backtrack. She checked her phone. Still plenty of time. She turned down the quiet lane and drove to the spot they'd found the day before. Bordered by tall fir trees, the old logging road was ideal for watching the compound. Rox drove down the dirt lane, then turned around, positioning herself as far from the main road as she could while still keeping the concrete buildings in sight.

Once she was settled in, Rox pulled out her binoculars and focused on the work camp. The Bronco was already gone. Blackstone had left early for his meeting with Loffland. What did that mean? That he had errands to run too? He didn't leave the complex often, so it made sense he would take advantage of his time in town. The white van was gone as well, leaving only the red minivan. Rox had expected the soup kitchen women to be gone, but she had hoped to get there in time to watch Blackstone leave. She decided to call Loffland just to see if this meet-up time had changed. Loffland didn't answer, so she left a message. Rox cursed herself for not checking with him earlier. Maybe it didn't matter. Blackstone had left the work camp. Step one accomplished.

If Marty was successful in commandeering a clinic phone, Margo would drive away soon too. But Rox would hear from Marty before that happened. Waiting for him to arrive would be tough. They might have only a short window of opportunity. Especially if Margo hit a Callback icon to get more information. Rox decided she would go for it the minute Margo drove away. Marty wouldn't like it, but he would already be on his way—only ten minutes or so behind. That might be all the time she had to get Emma out.

More worst-case scenarios played in her head. Margo would tell everyone where she was going, then Emma would be suspicious that her mother was having an emergency just as Margo's daughter was at urgent care. Or Margo would take Emma with her. Or maybe Margo would even lock up the girl somewhere while she was gone. That seemed extreme, but Emma never seemed to leave the complex. The only exception had been to go with Blackstone to collect the ten grand. These people were monsters, so anything was possible.

After another ten long minutes, Marty's ringtone sounded. Rox pressed her earpiece. "Yes?"

"I made the call, and Margo should be leaving in a few minutes. I'm headed your way now. Give me fifteen minutes." He laughed, a nervous sound. "If I don't get stopped for speeding."

"Be safe." She started to hang up, then said, "Hey, I wanted you to know Blackstone's Bronco wasn't at the complex when I arrived. So he left early."

"You saw him leave?"

Her gut clenched. "No. But considering everything we know about him, it's unlikely he let anyone else take his vehicle. I called Loffland but didn't get through."

Marty was quiet for a moment. "You're probably right. He might have left early this morning to do something else. We're going for it."

"Yes, but our window of opportunity could be limited. I'm going in as soon as Margo's car is out of sight."

"No! Wait for me!" Marty shouted. "The girls might be armed and dangerous. We have no idea of what we'll encounter."

His tone surprised her. He rarely got upset. But she was right about this decision. "The members won't be armed. And Margo might call the urgent care center or soup kitchen, then turn around and come right back. I might have only five minutes to get Emma out. I can't waste it sitting here."

"Shit!"

"It's okay. Margo might not be a problem anyway. Blackstone is the control freak." Rox heard an engine start and glanced over at the work camp. The minivan was backing out. "Margo's on the move. I have to go." She hung up and slouched down out of sight. The woman probably wouldn't even glance up the dirt road as she drove by, but Rox wanted to be safe. If the woman did, she would see an empty car and think *hiker* or *hunter*.

Rox counted while she waited just to keep her heart calm. This was it. She was going in to breach an old prison camp and conduct her ballsiest extraction yet. *And the CIA thought I couldn't do fieldwork.* The minivan passed at a high speed, and Rox waited for another full count of five, then sat up and started her engine. She drove to the paved lane and looked right. The car was in the distance, flying along. She pulled out and accelerated toward the work camp. For a moment, her mind was blank and she couldn't think at all. Then new ideas bombarded her. She had to act panicked at the door to be convincing. If Emma questioned her and mentioned Ronnie's emergency, Rox would say she knew about it. Then explain that Mrs. Carson had gone to the soup kitchen and she and Ronnie had been involved in an altercation that had injured both.

Stupid! None of this was well thought out. They'd rushed the execution and hadn't done enough preparation. But she kept driving. Blackstone was an abuser and possibly a killer. All of the girls were in danger, but Emma had become her responsibility. Once she'd been deprogrammed, the girl might be persuaded to press charges against the cult leader. It might be the only way to stop him.

Rox turned into the large gravel parking area and got her first up-close look at the work camp. A long, flat-roofed building with sun-faded concrete walls, no visible windows from the front, and a green metal door. Not a place that would be easy to call home. The flower planter on the front step was a pathetic attempt to soften the ugly edges. The perpendicular buildings in the back that she'd seen on the Google Earth map weren't visible from the parking area. She also spotted something new. A large metal shed had been added on the left of the main building since the photo had been taken. Its overhead door was up, and the Bronco was parked inside with the hood open.

Shit!

Blackstone, next to the vehicle, spun around when he heard the crunch of her tires on the gravel. In a quick move, he picked up a shotgun and charged toward her.

CHAPTER 20

Heart pounding, Rox threw her car in reverse and backed out. As Blackstone rushed toward her, he bellowed, "Why are you here?"

Could she salvage this? No, she had to leave and warn Marty to abort the mission. But first, she had to try to cover her tracks. Rox pressed the window button as she backed onto the road. When the window was down, she called out, "I'm with the US Census!"

"Don't come back!"

She rolled up the window and sped off. When she'd cleared his line of sight, she realized her legs were shaking. She wanted to pull off the road to call Marty but was afraid Blackstone might be following. Rox touched her earpiece, hoping for once to get the damn voice command to work. "Call Marty."

"Did you say, 'Call Mayfair Chiropractic'?"

What the hell? "No. Call Marty!" she yelled at the automated voice, even though it likely wouldn't help.

"Did you say, 'Call Marty'?"

"Yes!"

Her stepdad answered on the second ring. "What's happening?" He sounded as panicked as she felt.

"Blackstone was home, working on his Bronco. He was inside a garage, so I didn't see him or the vehicle from the logging road." Shame flooded her. Great operative she was. "I'm sorry."

"For what? Did something happen?"

"Well, he saw me pull in, for starters. I yelled that I was with the census, but we may have blown our only chance. He'll be paranoid now." Rox didn't want to tell Marty about the shotgun. Yet. She would if they found a way to try again.

"We can fix this." Marty was obviously trying to sound confident. "I'm turning around and going back to the urgent care place. I'll use the same phone and call Margo to tell her it was a mistake."

"That's sketchy."

"I know. But it's better than having her show up and know for sure that someone conned her."

"Agreed." Rox remembered they weren't the only ones involved. "I wonder why Loffland didn't warn me Blackstone had car trouble and canceled their meeting."

"Maybe he changed his mind about helping us."

Her thoughts were darker. "What if he betrayed me and told Blackstone I was coming?"

"Then you're right about us not getting another shot at breaching his home turf."

She remembered the look on the cult leader's face. "I don't know. Blackstone seemed surprised and asked what I was doing, so we might be okay."

"You want to try again?"

"I'm not giving up on Emma!" Rox realized she sounded more emotional than she'd intended.

Marty made a noise in his throat. "She's not Jolene. You can't save everybody."

"I know." Rox took a deep breath. "We just need a new idea."

"I need to hang up and drive like hell again."

"See you at home." Rox clicked off. *Damn!* She had really messed this up. Even if Marty pulled off another bullshit phone call, Margo would be confused, and Blackstone would be suspicious. Especially considering a census taker had supposedly stopped by moments after

Margo left. They might not get another shot at an invasive extraction. Poor Emma might be stuck in the cult until she became too old for Blackstone's taste. By then, her self-esteem would be devastated and she'd be so screwed up that her life might never be normal or happy. If she even lived. *Damn!* Rox pounded the steering wheel.

Deep breaths! She turned on to the main road and tried to calm herself. Just because they couldn't get inside the work camp didn't mean they couldn't try again. There had to be a way to get Emma out and separated from Blackstone. Marty might even be willing to pose as a cop and conduct a phony arrest. Maybe they should have done that in the first place. No, too risky. Blackstone might become violent, and Marty wouldn't have real police backup.

Even though her first instinct was always to blame herself, it was Loffland who had failed. The prick hadn't bothered to call and say his meeting with Blackstone had been canceled. Rox pulled off the road and punched Loffland's number into her burner phone. He answered right away. "Is this Karina?"

"Yes. What the hell? Why didn't you tell me Blackstone wasn't leaving the property?"

"I didn't know," he yelled back. "I'm sitting here in the tavern, waiting for him. I was just going to call you."

"About twenty minutes too late!" Taken aback by her own anger, Rox reined it in. "I'm sorry, but that could have gone badly. Blackstone keeps a shotgun at his side and doesn't like intruders."

"I'm sorry I waited to call. Are you okay?"

"Yes, but he'll be suspicious now, and we won't get another chance."

"Hey, I tried." His tone was nonchalant.

Rox started to sign off, then remembered their first conversation and the *incident* Loffland had mentioned. "Is there anything you know about Blackstone that I can use against him? Since we talked last, I discovered that he's physically abusing the girls, in addition to the sexual exploitation—"

Loffland cut in. "Son of a bitch."

Rox added, "If none of them will press charges or testify, there's nothing we can do legally. I need to get one girl out and deprogrammed to help bring him down."

For a long moment, Loffland was silent. "His father's in a nursing home, and it's costing a fortune, so Deacon needs money. Also, his dad is the only person on earth he gives a shit about."

A glimmer of hope. "What's his father's name?"

"I don't know. Hey, someone's calling me now." Loffland started to hang up, then added, "Arthur! I think the old man's name might be Arthur." The line went dead.

A nursing-home dad was the last thing she'd expected, but maybe they could work with it. Sun filtered in the window, and Rox looked up. The clouds were breaking apart, and chunks of blue dotted the sky. She started to feel optimistic again. They could do this. She put the car in gear and rolled onto the road.

Up ahead, she spotted the crappy trailer where Bethany's little blond boyfriend lived. No truck in the yard. Maybe she should stop in and see what else she could find out. She visualized the father coming home again. Having a gun pointed at her a third time in two days was more than she could handle. A phone call would be smarter. But she hadn't had time to give Noah one of her Karina Jones business cards before she left. What the heck? She would do that now. Rox hit the brakes and made a last-minute turn into the driveway, pulling off her wig as she parked.

As she walked up, business card in hand, Noah opened the door. "You shouldn't be here."

"I know. I just wanted you to have my phone number. In case you think of something important."

He blinked and seemed dazed.

"Bethany was murdered, and other girls are being abused. I need all the help I can get." She handed him the card.

He slipped it into his jeans pocket. "You'd better go."

Rox didn't need to be told.

When she arrived home, she texted Marty: *Let's update. Cold one on the deck.* She grabbed two bottles of beer and headed out back. A few minutes later, her stepdad came through the gate separating their backyards and joined her.

"What have you got?"

"Greg Loffland says Blackstone stood him up without even calling to cancel." She handed Marty a beer, and he sat in one of the canvas chairs.

"Do you believe him?"

"Maybe. He also told me Blackstone's father is in a nursing home and that it's costing him a fortune. Loffland mentioned it as a weakness we could use."

"Better than nothing. I'll try to find the place, even though I hate those slow-death corrals." He shuddered. "What's the old man's name?"

Marty had made her promise to kill him rather than put him in nursing home. She hoped to never actually face that moment. "It might be Arthur. I guess we assume they have the same last name. But how do we use that information?"

"We can't really fake another emergency, can we?" Marty tipped his beer back and let a long drink run down his throat.

"No, Blackstone is probably already suspicious. But apparently he loves his dad."

"We could kidnap the father and ask to trade him for the girl." Marty let out a rowdy laugh, seeming pleased with himself. "If the old man is senile, he might even go along."

Rox gave him a *get serious* look, then snapped her fingers. "Let's find out what kind of shape Arthur Blackstone is in. What if we can get the old man to call his son and ask for help?"

Marty rolled his head around, mulling the idea. "Maybe. Let me find the home first and get more information."

"Thanks. I think I'll go back out to the work camp to watch for a while. If the girls take off in the van, I might follow the crew again and see what I can find out."

Marty scowled. "I don't like that."

"We may have to stake out the complex for days and take turns."

A muffled pounding came from inside the house. They both jumped a little.

"That's the front door." Rox stood and hurried inside. Who could it be on Sunday? Some religious person with a pamphlet? As she approached, she heard a yell.

"Hey, it's Kyle!"

Rox opened the door, and her smile disappeared. He looked upset. "We're on the back deck and didn't hear you. Come in."

Kyle brushed past her, then turned and glared. "Were you wearing a nun's costume when you visited the soup kitchen on Wednesday?"

Damn! She didn't want to lie to him. "It doesn't matter. I went to the task force as soon as I heard she was dead and told your team I'd talked to her."

"What are you holding back?"

"Nothing. I want you to catch her killer."

He stood in the middle of the living room with crossed arms. "Why did you think Blackstone killed her?"

"He's a predator with a history of violence. What is this about?"

Marty slipped into the room behind them, and they both glanced over. Her stepdad stayed near the opening to the kitchen and didn't say anything.

Kyle finally looked back at her. "Did you know Bethany shot her father?"

Double damn. She hadn't updated him. "Not until yesterday. I'm sorry I didn't call you. But I didn't know it was important, and this has been an intense investigation."

Kyle crossed his arms. "What do you know about the trust fund?"

Bethany had money? "I don't know anything. How much is there? Enough for motive?"

Her boyfriend's body finally relaxed. "I don't know yet. It's a monthly royalty payment from her father's books that may only be a few thousand a month, and I don't know how Blackstone could get his hands on it."

"I'll bet he's trying. Thanks for telling me."

"You can't use that or share it." A flash of regret in his eyes.

"I'll keep it confidential." Rox stepped toward him, hoping he would soften. "I have a new update for you. Blackstone's father is in an expensive nursing home, and he's hurting for money."

"We'll look at Blackstone as a suspect again. Maybe we can break his alibi."

Marty spoke up. "I hope you'll share Bethany's financial info when you get it."

Kyle spun toward him. "Don't count on it." He shifted his gaze to Rox. "I want you to let this case go. Just give your client the money back and let us handle it. If Blackstone is dirty, we'll put him away, and all the members will be free to leave the property."

Rox bristled. He had no right to suggest it, and she had no intention of going along. "I'll think about it."

"Not good enough."

What the hell? Now she felt compelled to defend her position. "I want to shut down Blackstone too, but that could take months. Meanwhile, my client is worried about her child." Rox stepped toward the front of the house. "Nothing I do will interfere with your investigation." She opened the door. "I have to get back to work."

"You've changed, and not for the better." Kyle walked out without looking at her.

CHAPTER 21

Sunday, April 23, 10:30 a.m.

After breakfast cleanup, Emma went out to the barn. She hated the nasty poop and sweaty animal smells, but she needed to keep busy. Plus atone for yesterday. She'd been upset ever since she'd called her parents about the donation. Seeing her mother's heartache had made it worse. She wouldn't ever ask for money or agree to meet her again. She had enough guilt already. Deacon had promised to never pressure her for it again, and she prayed he would keep his word. He was a good man, and she trusted him, but the charity was still in trouble.

Emma grabbed a big shovel and started cleaning. After an hour, her hands were sore and blistered, but she continued until the pain made her cry. She sat on a bale of hay and tried to calm herself, but quickly got up. She had to get out of the barn. Outside, she breathed in fresh air, then headed into the dorm. As she hurried inside, she sensed that other members were in their own spaces, but with their curtains closed she was never sure. They were the quietest bunch of girls she'd ever been around.

Emma sat on her bed, wishing she liked to read like Skeeter did. The concrete walls and daily routines were getting on her nerves. Except for the stress of seeing her mother, going into town had been exhilarating! She wanted to work in the soup kitchen or go out and gather donations. Maybe Deacon would think she'd earned the privilege now that she'd brought in a lot of money for the charity. It wasn't the same as true good works, but it couldn't hurt to ask. Deacon had stressed the need for good mental health, and she was feeling restless.

She got up and headed to the wide entry, where she grabbed a pair of scrubs from the bin and headed for the shower to clean off the barn scent. If Deacon wanted to get close to her again, she needed to be fresh. She decided that if it would earn her off-campus privileges, she would have sex with him, like Bethany had. She wasn't saving herself for marriage or even a special boy. Those options had all disappeared the day she killed Marlee.

Later, as she dressed, another member walked toward her from her dorm space. "Showering in the middle of the day? What's that about?" Mona was twenty and went out at night with the donation crew. Her voice was low-pitched like an old smoker, and she had tattoo sleeves on both arms, but her face was striking.

Emma didn't know Mona's story and had been afraid to ask. "I've been cleaning the barn."

"Where are you going now?" Mona squinted down at her.

"Why?"

"You've been spending a lot of time with Deacon lately. I'll bet you're headed there now."

"So?" Emma stepped into her flip-flops, ready to walk away.

"Just remember, he likes it rough." Mona gave her an odd smile.

"What—" Emma didn't finish her question. She walked away rather than feel naive. Mona was talking about sex, of course. She was probably lying out of jealousy. Emma crossed the space between the buildings and entered the cafeteria. It was almost time to start cooking again, but this question couldn't wait. She hurried down the hall to Deacon's office and knocked. "It's Emma."

What if Mona was telling the truth? What did *rough* mean during sex? She had a vague idea from movies, but Deacon wasn't that kind of person. None of the other members who spent time with him had ever complained.

He opened the door, pulled her inside, and kissed her. The suddenness of it caught her off guard, and she stepped back.

A flash of disappointment and something else on his face. "You liked it last time I kissed you. What happened?"

"Uh, nothing. I was just surprised. And I wanted to ask you something."

He smiled, and the charm was back. "Okay then." He gestured for her to sit.

Emma slipped down to the couch, near the middle. He sat beside her and put his hand on her leg. "What did you want to ask?"

Emma swallowed hard, feeling apprehensive. "I want to work in the soup kitchen or maybe collect donations. I think I'm ready."

For a long moment, Deacon stared at her, then nodded. "I think you are too. You did great yesterday with your mother."

Emma cringed but tried to hide it. "Can I start tomorrow?" The Portland crew had already left the complex that morning.

"Why not tonight?" Deacon smiled. "You're too pretty for the soup kitchen, but you'll do well with the motorists."

Emma grinned. "Yay!" That meant she could change into real clothes that evening. "Do I need any kind of preparation?"

"Yes, but I'll let Mona handle most of it." He leaned in and kissed her again. Slowly this time. Emma's body responded, and she pressed into him. God, this felt good. She'd been so lonely. But she didn't deserve to feel good! Confused, Emma stopped kissing him but didn't pull back.

"Consider this training," Deacon said, still kissing her.

For what? Before she could ask, a knock interrupted them.

"God damn it!" Deacon stood and turned to the door. "Go away!"

"It's Margo, and it's important."

Deacon swore softly and moved behind his desk. He gestured at Emma to leave. "Go see Mona and tell her you're on the highway crew, but with a special mission. She'll know what I mean."

His impersonal tone stung. Was it because of Margo? Emma had thought the couple had an open relationship. As she stepped out, Margo gave her a quick nod and brushed past her. Was she jealous? Walking away, Emma had another realization. Deacon had been hiding his erection behind the desk. She giggled, covering her mouth to mute the sound. Boys were boys at any age.

A few minutes later, she was back in the dorm, standing outside Mona's space. She called softly, "It's Emma. Deacon wants you to train me."

After a rustling sound and a drawer closing, Mona pulled back the curtain and grinned. "That was fast." Her thin, angular body was well hidden by the too-big scrubs.

Emma flushed and shook her head. "Nothing happened. I asked to join your crew, and Deacon said yes." She straightened her shoulders, unashamed. "I can start tonight."

"So you're ready to get out of here?" Mona cocked her head. "But you left with Deacon a few days ago. What was that about?"

"A donation." Deacon had prepped her on what to say. So far, Mona was the only one who'd asked, although Emma had told Skeeter before she even left. It had been hard not to mention her mother.

"Hmm." Mona looked doubtful but reached out and grabbed her arm. "Come in and we'll get started."

Mona's space surprised her. She had a pretty blanket on her bed, a stuffed penguin near her pillow, and two bracelets on the dresser. None of those were allowed. The older girl noticed her staring at the jewelry and laughed. "The night crew has a few perks. As the crew leader and driver, I've earned them."

This layer of complexity confused her. "What about sacrifice and atonement?"

"My debt is paid." Mona stepped toward her. "Can I trust you?"

"Of course." How had she atoned? None of them deserved the good life.

The older girl leaned in and whispered, "I came here out of guilt, but I stay because this life makes more sense than the addiction and homelessness that waits for me out there."

The hopelessness in Mona's eyes crushed Emma's heart. *Poor girl.* "Don't you have a family?"

"They're either dead or gave up on me." Mona shrugged. "Let's get started." She hopped on the bed and sat cross-legged at the end near the wall. She gestured for Emma to join her.

Emma climbed on the bed, coveting the purple-and-black blanket. "What exactly do we do?"

"Simple. We ask strangers for money." Mona smiled. "Because it's for veterans, they usually give something." She reached for a stack of postcards and handed one to Emma. "We give these to people as we rattle off our spiel. They give the charity credibility. A few people read them, but most don't."

Emma was eager to interact with people and wanted to be good at bringing in money for the vets. "What's the spiel?"

"It's short and easy. You can practice on the way out tonight. Sometimes we have a long drive." Mona leaned back. "We'll role-play it once. Just go along."

"Okay."

"Do you support the troops?"

"Of course."

"What about when they return?"

"Yes."

"Many of our young soldiers are homeless now. Will you donate to our soup kitchen where we feed them seven days a week?"

"Of course." Emma smiled. "That's easy. It hardly needs training."

A distant look clouded Mona's eyes.

Emma started to ask what was wrong, then remembered what Deacon had said to mention. "I'm supposed to have a special mission."

Mona nodded. "Of course you are. You're a doll, and the bad boys will like you."

Bad boys? "What do you mean?"

"Oh fuck." The other girl was suddenly disappointed. "You really don't know?"

Emma felt naive again. "About what?"

Mona let out a long sigh. "Collecting a few dollars at a time won't even pay the lease on the soup kitchen, let alone buy food. So we ask some men to make big donations. Often in exchange for some breast grabbing or even a blow job."

Shocked, Emma recoiled. "That's prostitution."

The other girl shook her head. "They make a donation. You make them feel good." Her shoulders lifted a little. "And there are ways to get the money without blowing them."

Still reeling, Emma was afraid to ask. But it had to be better than giving blow jobs. "Like what?"

"You're not ready yet. Let's see how you do for a few nights."

"Where are we going?"

"We hit truck stops and rest areas along I-5. Tonight we're going south, almost to Salem."

Fear landed in the pit of Emma's stomach. "That seems dangerous."

Mona laughed. "You mean because of the serial killer?"

"Yeah, that."

The other girl gave her a sly smile. "I'm not his type, but you sure are."

CHAPTER 22

Deacon looked at Margo, trying to keep his face impassive. "Interrupting my sessions with Emma is counterproductive. Her parents have essential funding we need."

"I know. I'm sorry." She hurried into his office. "We have to talk about money."

"Right now?" *Was she wearing perfume?*

"Yes. I just realized that with Bethany gone, we'll be short her two grand this month. We need to pay the lease on the soup kitchen and skip the nursing home again."

Rage rippled up his spine. "I know that!" He didn't need her reminding him of their situation. "Your disregard for my father is so fucking cold."

She softened her expression. "Honey, it's not like that. I'm just trying to keep the charity going." Margo moved in close, pressing her body into his. "You need to chill, and I know how to help you relax."

She was wearing his favorite blouse, a tight red pullover with a deep V that showed off her cleavage. But he wasn't interested at the moment. Margo wasn't young and fresh, and he was highly agitated with her. Deacon stepped back. "You killed my mood. So unless we have further business to discuss, I'd like to get back to work." He'd been watching a movie, but that was beside the point.

Hurt and disappointment twisted into a sneer on her face. "What work? I hope it's finding a donation, because we're in deep shit if you don't." She strode out and slammed the door.

Bitch.

Deacon sat down and restarted the movie but couldn't focus on it. Too much shit was swirling in his head. Today had been weird. Margo had gotten a call from urgent care about her daughter being hurt, only to get another call twenty minutes later saying it had been a mistake. In between, a census taker had showed up at the complex. His gut told him it wasn't a coincidence. But what the fuck was it about? Someone was casing the place, and he had to think it was Greg. The asshole had tried to get him off the property today too. Was Greg setting him up? His so-called friend claimed he wanted to *work something out* with him. Deacon had planned to go have a beer with Greg, then changed his mind. He couldn't handle the pressure of any more demands for money.

God damn. He needed a big score, ASAP. Without it, he would have to abandon his dad and just say *fuck it*. Let the nursing home kick him out. What would they do? Roll the old man's wheelchair into the parking lot and say *adios*? No, they would dump him at a hospital. The heartless assholes. He couldn't do that. His dad didn't have much time left, and the old man counted on him. Disappointing him again right before he died wasn't in the cards. Deacon just needed enough money to keep the nursing home from shuffling the old man to a hospital, where he would die of neglect. Once he passed in the comfort of his own space, everything would settle back down.

Deacon got up to take a walk, but his phone rang. Greg again. *Fuck!* He decided to take the call, just to stall the blackmail bullshit until he got set up with a new phone number. If Greg couldn't reach him, he might just back off. Deacon wanted to believe his former friend would never actually follow through on his threat of exposure. Dozens of military personnel had profited from selling what they called *liquid gold.* It hadn't hurt the army, or anyone. And his combat pay had been laughable.

"Hello?" He wanted Greg to think he didn't recognize his number or have him in his contacts—as though he wasn't concerned.

"Deacon. What the fuck happened today?"

"My Bronco wasn't running well, and I had to work on it." He kept his tone casual.

"You could have called!" Greg's voice got louder. "And you've ignored my calls. You can't just avoid this. I want the god damn money!"

"I don't have it. You're wasting your time." He remembered the strange incidents earlier. "Why are you casing my property?"

"What?"

A freaky thought hit him. "Is this about Margo? Did you fake that call to lure her out for revenge sex?"

"You're a sick fuck."

Deacon let it go. Maybe it had been nothing. No one knew the charity's location. Not even the state office where they'd registered it for the tax-exempt status. They'd moved shortly after filing the paperwork and hadn't notified anyone. They kept in touch with their regular donors by email, and the fools sent checks to a post office box. He just had to get Greg to back off. "I don't have the cash you need and no way to get it, so just leave me the fuck alone."

"You have wealthy donors! Start making calls. I'll gladly report your theft if you don't come through." Greg let loose with a nasty laugh. "Even if the army doesn't strip you of your medals, your charity will go bankrupt from the bad publicity—and you'll lose your access to all those young girls. You have until four on Friday." He hung up.

Deacon stared at the phone. How did Greg know about the sisters?

CHAPTER 23

Rox parked on the same dirt road as she had that morning and shut off her car. The setting sun flickered through the trees, at first beautiful but slowly turning creepy. Rox listened to music to keep herself occupied, while she occasionally trained her binoculars on the work camp. She couldn't see much, but she was mostly hoping to notice headlights come on. She wanted the van to go out so she could track the girls and question one of the members. Casting some doubt about Blackstone among his followers could start a rumor that got back to Emma. Even a wedge of uncertainty might make it easier to gain the girl's cooperation—if they got another shot at connecting with her.

Rox didn't have to wait long. A group of girls came out the door and headed for the white van. A motion-sensor light came on, partially illuminating them. Rox recognized the tallest young woman from the truck stop the other night. Was that Emma walking next to her? Rox strained to tell. They were all slender, and several had long hair. In the distance and dim light, it was impossible to see. It also seemed unlikely, especially after the events of the day. Rox texted Marty anyway: *Emma may be on the move. Be on standby.*

In the distance, the van's engine rumbled, and Rox started her vehicle, eager to get moving. Would the girls return to the same truck stop, or did they move around? They probably had a dozen or so places along the highway where they solicited. She hoped she didn't lose them in the dark freeway traffic. A count of ten after the van passed, then Rox eased forward and onto the road. The lack of homes and cars out here might make it obvious to the driver that she was being followed. Rox had to be careful.

Rox hung back until the van neared the 205 highway's entrance, then moved in closer. As expected, more traffic pulled onto the road and took up the space between her and the van. The vehicle went west again toward I-5, taking the south exit again. She followed the van for twenty-five miles to a truck stop north of Salem and parked in the motel lot across the access road. This gas station–restaurant combo was smaller than the first one and had only a dozen or so big rigs. Yet the front parking lot was full of small SUVs, the new family car.

Through binoculars, Rox watched the Sister Love members climb out of the van. Emma was with them! Her narrow face and white-blonde hair were distinctive. A tremor of excitement rushed up Rox's spine. Their x-target was fully accessible. Maybe they could pull this off tonight and be done with it. She grabbed her phone and called Marty, noticing he hadn't texted back. Her stepdad didn't pick up. *Damn!* He was probably watching TV and had the volume up full blast as usual.

She left a message, her voice more urgent than she intended. "I'm at Jackman's, the gas station and café on I-5 north of Salem. Emma is here with the Sister Love girls. Maybe we can grab her tonight." Rox glanced in the binoculars again. The girls were headed inside the restaurant. "I'll give Emma the *mom-emergency* bullshit to get her in the car, then hope for the best. I could use some backup." She started to sign off, then added, "Text, please, instead of call. I don't want my phone going off if I'm in proximity."

Rox put on glasses and a baseball cap, then climbed out of her car. Without a gift shop, this truck stop offered no real place to hang back and watch, but she needed to get in close. She crossed the road and entered the parking lot, an eerie sense of déjà vu hanging over her.

The lurker from the last truck stop flashed in her mind, and she automatically looked around. Spotting only one older man sleeping in a passenger seat, she moved forward. That incident had been a fluke and probably had nothing to do with the Sister Love crew.

Rox stepped into the restaurant and looked around. The girls had split up like before, and Emma was sitting with the dark-haired girl who'd gotten into the truck last time and seemed to be the leader of the crew. *Damn.* A sense of urgency overcame Rox. She needed to get Emma out before the girl started down a path toward prostitution. Rox stepped back outside. She needed a plan. She needed Marty. He could approach Emma and pretend to be interested in the charity. Maybe get her to come outside. She called him again, and this time he answered. "What's the update?"

"You didn't see my text or listen to my message?"

"No, sorry. I've been watching a game."

Rox ran down the situation. "It'll take you nearly thirty minutes to get here, but I'll try to wait. You have a better shot at getting her away from the cluster than I do."

"Hang tight. I'm on my way."

Rox walked to the end of the building, leaned against the wall, and stared at her cell phone. How long could she pretend to be a motorist taking a break? Holding back wasn't in her nature. If Emma walked out the door with a man and headed for a big truck, Rox would move in.

After ten minutes, a family with small children left the restaurant, followed by an older couple shortly after. Rox paced to the front entrance, resisted the urge to go inside, then headed back to her spot near the corner. She heard the door again and turned back. A fifty-something man with a squat build stepped out, and the dark-haired cult member with tattoos followed. Rox watched them walk into the truckers' parking area and climb into the second rig. Curious as she was about what the cult members really did in exchange for donations,

Rox stayed put. She wasn't going to miss Emma if she exited the café. Still, Rox glanced back and forth between the restaurant door and the big truck. She'd developed a concern for all the sisters. After hearing Bethany's backstory, in addition to Emma's, she now realized that most of the members were deeply damaged—and becoming more fucked up as they did Blackstone's bidding.

Motion in the cab of the big rig caught her eye. Oh shit! The trucker was punching Tattoo Girl in the face and now had her pinned against the door.

Rox charged toward the semi-trailer, reaching for the weapon she no longer carried, her Glock still in her car. She rejected the idea of using it anyway. A loud interruption might be enough to intimidate the prick. As she neared the truck, she shouted, "Hey! Leave her alone!"

The round-faced man turned his head, startled, and stared at her through the high windshield. The girl had all but disappeared under him.

Rox shouted again. "Let her go!"

The trucker mouthed nasty things in her direction.

Rox slammed her palm into the passenger door. "I'll call the cops!" She heard him yell, "Bitch," and the door opened. Rox jumped back, and Tattoo Girl tumbled to the ground. Rox squatted and grabbed her by the shoulders. "Let's get you out of here."

The dark-haired girl pushed to her feet. "I'm fine."

Rox ignored her, and pulled her away from the truck. Jolene had become a sex slave to the man who controlled her life and had put up a tough front too. This girl needed help. But Tattoo Girl pulled free. "Get away from me."

Rox let her go and glanced at the restaurant door. Nothing was happening. But she'd taken her eye off it for five minutes. To reassure herself, Rox hurried inside the café and looked around. Where was Emma? *Shit!* How could she be gone? Maybe she was in the restroom. Rox strode to the side hallway, her speed and anxiousness feeling obvious and out of place. A table of truckers looked up at her as she passed. The space and both stalls in the restroom were empty. She ran back outside. Had Emma climbed into a truck too? *Damn!*

Rox scanned the row of big rigs, not seeing anyone in the cabs. But most big trucks had sleeping compartments. Emma could be on her back and out of view. Rox spun toward the other parking area. She had to check it first. Before what? Going back to pound on every big truck, calling out Emma's name?

Jogging to the front lot, Rox passed Tattoo Girl, who was smoking a cigarette by the front door. The girl called out, "Who the fuck are you?"

Rox kept moving. A car pulled out of the gas station nearby, and it was loaded with young men. Please don't let her be in there. Movement in the space between the two buildings caught her eye. A young girl was walking toward the tiny convenience store inside the gas station. Emma!

Rox stepped up her pace. This was perfect. Emma was alone, out of the complex, and hopefully open to outside influence. As Rox closed the gap, someone in a dark trench coat stepped out of a small car and grabbed the girl—holding a hand across her mouth.

What the hell?

Rox sprinted forward, shouting, unaware of the actual words she formed. The attacker turned, their face covered by a dark ski mask with a contrasting neck band. The sight of it made her heart skip a beat. "Let her go!" She screamed it so loudly her throat hurt.

The assailant shoved Emma aside, scrambled back into the car, and punched the gas of the still-idling engine. The small vehicle came straight at her, and Rox jumped out of the way, tripping and stumbling into a pickup truck. Her body slammed hard, and the impact knocked the wind out of her. Footsteps raced by as she processed the pain. When Rox caught her breath, she looked around. Where was Emma now?

Rox scanned the area and saw the girl running for the white van. The other sisters were piling in too. *Damn!* Rox wasn't surprised to see them go. It had been a rough night, and they were clearing out. But she couldn't let this opportunity slide. "Emma! Stop! I have something to tell you." The girl glanced her way but climbed through the side door of the van. The engine started, and the vehicle lurched forward.

Damn! Rox spun back toward the side road, hoping to get another look at the vehicle the assailant was driving. But all she saw were taillights heading up the freeway ramp.

CHAPTER 24

Monday, April 24, 9:05 a.m.

Detective Kyle Wilson glanced at his cell phone. The team meeting was taking forever, and the sergeant in charge hadn't called on him yet. The medical examiner had already taken up a chunk of their time and was still talking about the forensic evidence from Bethany Grant's murder. There seemed to be a lack of anything to compare to the other deaths, and Kyle's mind was on the victim's finances.

Abruptly the bearded ME said, "The ligature marks on the neck were interesting though."

Wilson snapped to attention.

"On the surface, they look like the other I-5 cases and were most likely made with a piece of cloth, a thick scarf, or belt. But Bethany Grant's bruising was less severe, and the hyoid bone wasn't damaged. Either this girl struggled less than the others, or the killer was physically weaker." The medical examiner gave a small shrug. "But I can't conclude for certain that the murder was committed by a different killer. People have off days. If our perp is a drug user, he could have been less high, or even straight, that day."

Wilson wanted more clarity. "But it's possible that it was a copycat crime?"

"That's what I'm saying."

The sergeant started to speak, but Wilson cut him off. "This seems like a good time to mention that I found another motive for Grant's murder."

"You have the floor." The sergeant's tone held a note of sarcasm.

"I talked to one of the workers at the Sister Love kitchen. She told me Grant had shot and killed her father accidentally and had probably moved here from Eureka. So I called the PD there." Wilson paused to sip his coffee—two weeks without a day off was taking its toll. "They informed me that the father had been an author and that his royalties were still going into a trust for his daughter. The Eureka detective is trying to locate the financial information and will fax it to me when he does. I expect it this morning."

The sergeant glanced at him over black-rimmed glasses. "How much money are we talking about?"

"I'm not sure yet. Maybe a couple grand a month."

"Enough to kill for." The sergeant made a note on the whiteboard and turned back. "But only if the killer could access the funds. Trusts are written by lawyers and are usually very specific and hard to break."

"I know," Wilson said. "It's a long-shot idea. Plus, it would have to be someone close to her. Bethany had no other family." He thought about Deacon Blackstone and the work camp full of women. "Other than the cult members, I mean."

"Get the bank records, then update me." The sergeant turned to another detective. "What did you learn about the tire marks at the last scene?"

"We found three sets, and none matched the evidence from any of the murders." Detective Sabine shook his head. "But the sets from the second crime scene were inconclusive as well."

The sergeant used his wrap-up voice. "I don't have to point out that the time frame between each of these murders is getting shorter. Based on the pattern, we can expect him to strike again any night."

A deputy from the sheriff's office stood and said, "We've added highway patrols, but the geographic area is so expansive, I'm not sure it will make a difference."

"We do what we can." The sergeant put down his whiteboard pen. "Keep me updated, and we'll meet again on Wednesday."

The other ten law enforcement officers stood and filed out. Wilson hurried to his cubicle on the second floor, grateful that he didn't have to drive to the meetings like many of the other team members. The Portland PD had taken the lead on the cases because the first body had been dumped inside the city limits.

At his desk, he checked his email. The Eureka detective had sent a message with several documents attached. Wilson downloaded and printed the files, eager to see what had been coming and going from the Grant trust each month.

He walked over to the shared printer and snatched up the papers, which were still shooting out. Damn, more reading than he'd expected. He glanced through the first few pages. It was all legal mumbo jumbo about how the trust was set up. He would get the details of that later. Right now he wanted to know how much the monthly royalties were and whether they had gone, or were going into, the Sister Love bank account.

After scooping up the rest of the papers from the printer tray, he strode back to his desk. The other cubicles were mostly empty or the detectives were quietly doing what he was—reading and analyzing documents.

Thirty minutes later, he had a summary. Barrett Grant had been earning a monthly average of $2,300 around the time of his death, and it had gone into an account called Grant Family Trust at Pacific Crest Bank. But these were old documents, and things could have changed in the last year. Wilson called the Eureka branch of the bank, identified himself, and asked to speak to a manager. He was transferred to a young woman named Ariel. He launched right in. "Your customer, Bethany

Grant, who inherited the Grant Family Trust, has been murdered, and I need your help."

"Oh no. That's terrible." She was quiet for a moment. "That poor family. Her father died just a year ago."

"I'm aware of the circumstances. I need to know what has happened to the royalties since Bethany inherited the trust."

"I don't know if I'm allowed to tell you that. I'd better ask my boss."

"Bethany is dead. You're not violating her confidence, but you would be helping find her killer."

"Uh, okay. Do you want me to send the account statements?"

"Please." He gave his email, assuming they would come as PDFs. "Can you open a couple of the statements right now and summarize for me?" Sometimes people got busy and forgot to follow through. He needed basic information ASAP.

"Let me pull up the account."

A moment later she mumbled, "It looks like Bethany made monthly cash withdrawals from her local branch for the full amount of the royalty, leaving a balance of around a thousand, from month to month."

"What's the average amount of the royalties deposited?"

"It varies. In February, they were around twenty-five hundred, but last month, it was only seventeen hundred and thirty."

The downward trend wasn't surprising, considering the author had died. "Where do the royalties come from?"

"Amazon dot com and few smaller ones from Audible."

"Has money left the account in the last week?"

"No."

"When is the next royalty due?"

"Hmm. Let's see if there's a pattern." A pause. "Of course. They come at the end of each month on the twenty-sixth or twenty-seventh."

In the next few days. Would someone try to pull out the cash? Could they? "Is anyone on the account besides Bethany?"

"No."

"Can you freeze the trust? So no one can access the money?"

"I don't know." She sounded skeptical. "I'll try to find out. We might need a court order."

That could take days. "Hey, if someone tries to access the money, I need you to call me."

A long pause. "If it's a cash withdrawal from another branch, I'll have no knowledge of that."

He would have to find and call the bank closest to the work camp. "Who is Bethany's heir?"

"I have no idea. You'd have to ask her lawyer."

The girl probably didn't have one, unless her father's lawyer was still involved with the trust. "What happens to the money if she has no heir?"

"It probably just sits there. But I'll see what I can find out. Can I call you back about that?"

"Thank you. Don't forget to send the monthly statements."

"Right. I will."

Wilson hung up. The only thing he didn't know was what Bethany had done with the cash every month. But he would have bet his own paycheck that it had ended up with Deacon Blackstone. Did Rox know? Was that what she was holding back? He didn't want to ask her and risk being lied to. He still cared enough to be hurt by a betrayal. The only way to find out for certain about the money was to subpoena the charity's bank statements. Blackstone's personal accounts too, if they were separate.

Time to go see a judge.

CHAPTER 25

Monday, April 24, 8:35 a.m.

Rox woke after a night of bad dreams and poor sleep and dragged herself to the kitchen to make coffee. This case was affecting her peace of mind. She couldn't think about anything else, yet she was making no progress in getting Emma out of the cult. Something had to break their way. Such as Marty finding the nursing home where Arthur Blackstone stayed, and the old man being senile enough to help them.

She sat down with her coffee and cereal and skimmed the front page of the Portland newspaper. One story contained updates on the I-5 Killer case and mentioned the escalating frequency of the murders. She thought about the night before, and a shudder quivered through her. Had she stopped Emma from being the killer's fifth victim? It seemed unlikely, but who else would wear a ski mask and grab a young girl at a truck stop? She'd called Kyle the night before and left him a message about the incident, but now she wondered if that was enough. He might not be listening to his voice mails again. She'd also reported the incident to the state sheriff's office. But once the desk officer realized the victim and the assailant were both gone from the truck stop, he'd lost interest in sending a deputy out to the scene. Rox had promised to file a report online but hadn't done it yet.

She ate the last of her Mini-Wheats and showered before calling Kyle again. She expected him to give her crap for being at the truck stop, especially after asking her to back off the case. He'd been so upset with her yesterday! But damn, she was a private investigator, and it was her job. He'd never complained about her activities before. But they'd never had an overlap. Still, none of her cases had ever felt this dangerous. She pressed Kyle's contact icon and waited, expecting it to go to voice mail, even hoping it would.

But he picked up. "Hey, Rox. Sorry about yesterday. I might have overreacted."

"You did." She decided to be gracious. "But it's okay. I know you're stressed about the I-5 investigation."

"I've also been working twelve- and fifteen-hour days for two straight weeks."

"Good grief. I didn't realize it had been that bad. When do you get a break?" She almost didn't want to tell him about the truck stop incident now. He would feel compelled to follow up.

"I don't know. But let's have dinner tonight. My treat."

"I'd like that." Rox hesitated. "Did you listen to your messages?"

"Only from my sergeant."

"Then I have something that might make you change your mind about dinner."

"More Sister Love crap?"

Rox bristled. "I'm going to tell you anyway." She took a breath to calm herself. "I was working my case last night and followed the charity van to a truck stop just north of Salem. First, one of the girls was assaulted by a trucker; then my clients' daughter was grabbed by someone in a trench coat wearing a ski mask. I interfered, and the assailant drove away, almost running me over. What if it was the I-5 Killer?"

"That's crazy! Did he hurt you?"

"Nothing serious." She kept her tone clipped, still a little upset with him.

"What are these girls involved in?"

Rox wondered that too. But it was beside the point. "Does the trench coat and ski mask fit the killer's profile at all?"

"We've never had an eyewitness describe him." A long pause.

"Is there something you're not telling me?"

"I just found out, and it isn't something I should share."

"Is this about Sister Love? I need all the information I can get." She didn't remind him that he'd already given her confidential information.

"Without going into detail . . ." He trailed off, then said softly, "Bethany withdrew a couple thousand from her trust account every month in cash."

No surprise. "I think Blackstone is selective about who he recruits. My clients have money too, and Blackstone has milked them for it." Rox suddenly realized what Kyle was thinking. "The money creates a motive for Blackstone—if he has a way to access the trust."

"Exactly." She heard him clicking his keyboard for a moment, then he added, "But we'll look at last night's incident. Tell me everything you noticed about the assailant, including the make of the vehicle."

"A little shorter than me, so maybe five-nine. Average-size body under the coat. The hood was up, and he had on a ski mask, so I don't have much else for description. And it was dark." Rox tried to visualize the vehicle that had almost hit her, but she'd been distracted at the time with trying to save her own life. "I'm not sure about the car. Something smaller and boxier than the family cars everyone is making now. So it was probably at least ten or twelve years old. And not a light color either—something mid-range."

"That's semi-helpful." His tone was slightly mocking.

"Hey, it was dark and he tried to run me over. I wasn't processing details."

"Fair enough."

Her worry finally all came together in a coherent thought. "If the I-5 Killer murdered Bethany and came after Emma, he might be targeting the Sister Love girls. I think you guys should start watching the truck stops where they solicit donations." That would effectively stop her from questioning the cult members in that crew. But their safety came first. That was the whole point of her case.

"Do you think Blackstone is the serial killer?"

She'd considered it. "I don't know. I'm not sure he fits the typical profile."

"Me neither, but I'll update the team and see what our profiler thinks."

"Are we still on for dinner tonight?"

"Maybe. I'll be in touch."

"See you later."

"Rox, be careful, please."

"I will." Rox hung up, glad he hadn't asked about her case or what she had planned. Not that she would tell him—for his own sake.

A moment later, Marty knocked and came through her door without waiting for her to respond. "I found the nursing home *and* learned that Arthur Blackstone has dementia." He was clearly excited. "If we can get the old guy to call his son and sound troubled enough to lure him out, I think we could take another run at the cult today."

She jumped up at the thought. "Are we ready? What if Margo is there?"

"We'll deal with it. She might be as passive as the other followers." Marty paced the room. "I think the longer we wait, the more guarded Blackstone will be." He glanced at Rox with a worried expression. "After what happened last night, I think Emma is in serious danger. We have to get her out today."

Her conversation with Kyle was fresh in Rox's mind. "I just learned that Bethany had monthly access to cash, so now Kyle is looking at

Blackstone as a suspect in her murder. Another reason to move in before Blackstone walls off himself *and* the girls."

Marty stopped in front of where she stood. "Maybe you should go to the nursing home and let me handle the extraction."

She knew he was worried about weapons. "I'll be fine."

He shook his head. "If anything happens, it's better that I take the hit, either physically or legally."

"This is my business." She grinned to take the sting out of her words. "You work for me as a contractor."

"That's bullshit." He laughed. "None of that matters. We actually need both of us to go in."

"Agreed. But how—" Rox stopped. They had one other option. "I'll call Greg Loffland and see if he'll help us again. He might even know Blackstone's father better than he indicated."

Marty looked skeptical. "Do you trust him? Especially after yesterday?"

"I think so." She moved toward her phone. "I'll meet him at the nursing home and coach him on the call. Then he'll need to give me twenty minutes to drive like hell to the work camp. This time, you'll be waiting and watching for Blackstone to leave."

"This could work." Marty bounced on his feet, a sign of nervousness she hadn't seen in a while.

"*If* Loffland is available. And willing. And doesn't screw us over." Rox shrugged, put her phone on speaker, and made the call.

Loffland answered. "Karina?"

"Yes. We think our client is in danger, and we want to try again today to extract her. Will you help?"

"I'm kind of busy with paperwork this morning, and I have to show a house this afternoon. Can it wait until tomorrow morning?"

"No. The police think Blackstone might have murdered Bethany Grant, one of his members."

"Why would he do that?" A deadpan tone.

"Because she had money, and he wanted it."

"He is in financial trouble." A brief pause. "But I don't see him as a killer."

She disagreed. "Even so, he's abusive, and we're all concerned." Rox knew she should call and update the Carsons, but she didn't want to mention the attack at the truck stop. It would just worry them more. She wanted to wait until she had Emma in her car and good news to report. She realized Greg needed motivation. "I'll pay you for your time. I sometimes hire outside help anyway."

"How much?"

"For an hour? Three hundred dollars."

"Not worth it."

"Come on. Young girls are being physically and sexually abused. We need to get our client out, get her deprogrammed, and help her file charges."

A long hesitation this time. "I want a thousand bucks. I have some financial needs of my own."

Rox looked at Marty. He nodded, and she knew he would say to take it out of his pay. They both knew she wouldn't.

"Okay. I'll give you a grand. Meet me at the Linnwood Care Facility in Clackamas in half an hour."

Another hesitation. "What's the plan?"

"You have to get Blackstone's senile father to call his son and ask him to come to the nursing home."

"How the hell am I supposed to pull that off?"

"I have some ideas." For a thousand bucks, Loffland needed a better attitude. "Do you know Arthur Blackstone?"

"No."

"You served with his son, so wear your uniform. He'll respect you and do whatever you ask him to."

"What if Deacon doesn't fall for it?"

"Call him and be insistent. You tried to meet with Blackstone yesterday; try again." A few things suddenly clicked for her. "I suspect you have your own agenda with Blackstone. Work that angle if you have to. Just get him the hell out of the work camp for a while."

"I need a little more time. I can meet you in an hour."

Rox decided to give him some extra motivation. If he failed his mission, he wouldn't get full pay. That's how her fee was set up. But for now all she said was, "For a thousand bucks, you'd better come through."

CHAPTER 26

Rox paced in front of the nursing home, watching a transport-van driver load an elderly woman into a wheelchair. The hydraulic lift was slow, but it got the job done. The thought of being confined to a wheelchair made her shudder. But she refused to think about getting old. She caught her reflection in the window. She'd picked up some blue scrubs like the Sister Love clan wore—hoping it would make Emma trust her—and put on the blonde wig again, because that's what Loffland was expecting. A *Nurse Jackie* effect.

Where the hell was Loffland? One hour and sixteen minutes had passed since their phone conversation. Was he blowing her off? She started to doubt whether she could trust him. Military buddies were usually loyal to each other for life. But Loffland had an attitude about Blackstone—

A truck pulled into the lot, and she stared at the driver. *Yes!* That was the shaved-head man she'd met at the tavern. Rox relaxed and leaned against the wall in the covered entry area, reflexively touching the shoulder bag where she'd tucked the cash.

As he approached, she took the offensive. "You're late."

"I told you I needed an hour." He gave her a dirty look. "Who cares? I'm here."

Yes, and it was time to get on with it. "I called, and Arthur Blackstone is accessible to visitors now. But you'll have to check in with the front desk."

"Show me the cash."

She'd expected that and pulled out both bundles. "I'll give you the three hundred up front. But you have to earn the rest." She displayed the big payment and handed him the smaller packet.

He shoved it into his jacket pocket. "As soon as Deacon leaves the property, I want the rest."

Not possible. "I can't waste any of our access time backtracking to pay you. But as soon as I have the girl and we're free of the complex, I'll call you with a time and place to meet."

His eyes narrowed while he considered it. "Okay. Let's get this over with."

"What are you going to say?"

"Just let me handle it."

Why couldn't he tell her? "I want to know."

He gave her another look that she guessed was supposed to be intimidating. "I've known Deacon Blackstone for ten years, but I don't know his father or how far gone he is. I may have to play this by ear. It could take some time. But Deacon loves his dad, and I will get him here."

She hated not being in control of this element, but her only other choice was to go in with him, and that might be overwhelming to the old man and make the objective harder. By leaving now, she could be in position for the extraction early. Rox gave him a thumbs-up. "A dozen young girls will benefit from this, so go. And call me as soon as you have an update."

Loffland walked away, pressed the security buzzer, and entered the nursing home. She waited until she saw the receptionist leading him down a hallway, then hurried to her car. Now that things were finally in motion, she had to call the Carsons again. They had been devastated when yesterday didn't work out. Jenny didn't answer, so Rox left a brief message. "Karina here. We're trying again soon. Be ready." She started her vehicle and accelerated out of the parking lot.

Even though she had more time to reach the work camp than she'd originally planned, she still pushed the speed limit and got to the rendezvous spot in twenty minutes. Marty waited in his sedan next to the big fir tree, looking surprised to see her. Rox switched cars, talking as she climbed in. "I left Loffland on his own, but I think he'll come through."

"Or we could be sitting here all day for no reason."

"That's the nature of this business."

"But you trust Loffland." Half statement, half question.

"Sort of." She shrugged. "I'm not sure we have a choice."

"There's always a choice." Marty switched to his wise-cop voice. "We can walk away from this if anything seems hinky."

"Of course, but let's try to plan."

"Right." Marty turned in his seat to face her. "We go in with one car, correct? So as we exit, I drive and you control the girl."

"Yes, and we take her straight to her parents. We'll pick up my car later."

"Are the Carsons ready?"

"I hope so. They've been on standby since yesterday."

"Are they taking her to a treatment center?"

"No, they've hired a deprogrammer who will come to them. That way Emma can stay in her own home and feel comfortable—while still getting the same level of treatment."

"That has to be quite spendy."

"She's lucky. Their money probably kept her out of jail for manslaughter too."

"I'll bet the parents of the dead girl sued them for a chunk of it."

"They never mentioned it." Rox's phone rang, and she snatched it up. *Greg Loffland.* "What's the update?"

"I convinced the old man he was being mistreated, and he called Deacon to report it. He should be on his way to give the staff hell."

Yes! "Thank you. I'll call in a few hours about the rest of your payment." Rox hung up before he could make any demands. She turned to Marty. "We should see Blackstone leave any moment."

"Great. Which strategy will you use?"

"I plan to keep it simple. Emma's mother is sick and needs to see her daughter."

"Take your Glock." He'd said it a few times already that morning.

"No. I'm not shooting anyone, and neither are you. But if I'm not out in ten minutes, you come in."

"I'd rather go in with you."

They'd already had this conversation as well. "You'll intimidate the girls, and I need you to watch for Blackstone."

"I know." Marty stiffened. "I'll keep an eye out for Margo too. Her minivan is gone right now, so she could come home in the middle of all this."

Rox couldn't worry about Margo. They just had to go for it. An engine roared, and they both snapped their heads toward the complex. The Bronco threw gravel as it backed out and turned to the road.

"He looks pissed." Rox laughed, but it made her nervous.

"As long as he stays away so we can get this done."

"He will. I figure we've got at least forty-five minutes."

Through the trees, they watched the Bronco fly down the highway. After a count of ten, Rox said, "Let's do this."

Marty drove forward and eased onto the road, turning in the opposite direction Blackstone had driven. "Good thing Margo's not home. She might be suspicious of another medical emergency." Marty's voice was quiet and hurried, as though talking to himself.

He was nervous. She patted his arm. "This will work out. It's just a few timid young girls in there." But Rox had her own apprehensions. Even young women with low self-esteem could be taught to use weapons to defend what they'd been taught was their home and family.

They drove down the road a short ways, pulled into the gravel lot, and parked in front of the long concrete building. The little silver-blue car she'd seen once was the only vehicle in the lot.

"Who drives that?" Marty asked, just as she wondered the same thing.

"It must be Ronnie's, Margo's daughter. I saw her with it at the soup kitchen."

"Ready?"

She and Marty looked at each other for a long moment. They didn't have to say anything. They loved each other and would do anything to protect the other.

As Rox stepped out, Marty mumbled, "Remind me to tell you something after this."

She glanced back, surprised, but didn't ask. Now was not the time to be distracted with his girlfriend news, or whatever it was. Rox hurried to the green door, mentally prepping for the role she had to play. Upset and worried didn't come naturally to her. Could she pull this off? She pressed the buzzer and waited.

It took three minutes, but Ronnie finally came to the door. "What do you want?"

Rox hoped the young woman didn't recognize her. She'd worn her hair in a bun and reading glasses when they'd talked at the soup kitchen that second time. "I have to see Emma Carson. I'm her mother's caregiver. Jenny Carson is deathly ill and needs her daughter."

Ronnie pressed her lips together. "How did you find us?"

"Her mother hired somebody. She's dying and desperate." Rox moved forward, crowding into the homely woman's personal space. "What's your name?"

"Ronnie." She stepped back, probably not even realizing she was doing it. "What's yours?"

Rox realized she couldn't use Karina Jones again. "Jolene." She crossed the threshold. *She was inside!* "Where is Emma?"

Panic flashed in Ronnie's eyes. "You shouldn't be in here." The woman tried to crowd her back out the still-open door, but Rox slipped around her and surveyed the room. They hadn't done much with the lobby of the work camp, except to remove whatever reception counter might have existed. A couch and a few chairs lined the walls, but there was no TV, no magazines, and no young girls. The room branched off into main hallways going in both directions, with a door in the middle of the back wall. Was a communal living space beyond this room? Rox wanted to be smart about her search and keep her time in the complex to a minimum.

"I have to see Emma. Where is she?" Rox kept moving toward the door in the back wall. She suspected the buildings behind this one were dorms and that she might find Emma and the other girls out there.

Ronnie closed the gap and grabbed Rox by her shoulder. "I'll go get Emma. You need to stay here."

Rox pulled free, yanked open the interior door, and stepped through. Two industrial table-bench combinations sat in the middle of a large cafeteria with a kitchen on the left. She spotted large stainless-steel appliances through a pass-bar. Windows along the back wall filled the sparse room with natural light. Beyond the glass, she spotted a greenhouse and a concrete bunker. Voices in the kitchen caught her attention, so Rox hurried through the swinging door. A slender blonde girl at the sink turned to face her. Emma!

"Hello, Emma. Your mother is very sick and needs you to come home."

Confusion played on the girl's face. Even without makeup, she was pretty in a doll-like way. "I saw you last night at the truck stop."

"I know. I saved you from an attacker."

"Why are you following me?" Emma's confusion morphed into suspicion and anger.

Damn. This wouldn't be easy. "Because I'm trying to get a message to you that your mother is sick and needs you." Rox went straight for the heart. "She might be dying. You don't want to miss your chance to say good-bye."

Emma crossed her arms. "I don't believe you."

Rox kicked herself for not faking some kind of proof.

Emma added, "She would have told me when I saw her the other day."

Rox was ready for this. "She planned to break it to you easy. But Deacon didn't give her enough time. He bolted with you as soon as he got the money."

Ronnie was suddenly in the middle of the conversation. "What money?"

CHAPTER 27

Wild thoughts bounced around Deacon's head. He would find the bitch who'd been abusing his father and give her a taste of her own bullshit. Better yet, he would keep his calm, get more information, and sue the fucking place for millions. That would solve a lot of issues, including getting Greg Loffland off his back. The son of a bitch really expected him to fork over twenty grand so he and that cunt, Kerry, could have a baby. If the charity could score a donation—or if he won a million-dollar lawsuit—he would pay Greg just to shut him up about the fuel scam.

Deacon slowed for the turn on Barton Road, then hit the accelerator. It was unusual to be leaving the complex again so soon after weeks of peaceful seclusion. First he'd taken Emma to get cash from her mother, then he'd almost left to meet with Loffland yesterday, and now he was on the road again. No wonder he was so irritable.

Margo was getting on his nerves too, with her constant complaining about money, then bitching about his seduction of Emma, even though she knew it was an effort to secure financing. A thought hit him, and he eased off the gas. Margo had been called out yesterday by an urgent care doctor about her daughter—which had turned out to be a mistake. Now he was headed to the nursing home. Was something going on after all? But his dad had made the call, not some doctor, and the old man had sounded upset. Still, he *was* senile, and this was starting to feel like a pattern. Did someone want him and

Margo gone from the complex? She wasn't home right now either. The members were alone.

Deacon braked and looked for a place to pull off the road. He needed to call his dad and ask a few questions if he could. Maybe he would even talk to a staff member and see if anyone had visited his father that morning. *Fuck!* Had he been conned?

CHAPTER 28

Before Rox could respond, Emma turned to Ronnie and said, "My mother made a donation, that's all. And I'm not sure this is your business."

A rift between the two members? That could only help her cause. Rox stepped toward Emma, wanting to be close enough to grab her if necessary, then turned to face the older girl. "Yes, please give us a minute of privacy."

"I don't trust you." Ronnie glared at Rox with crossed arms.

Emma reached out and touched Ronnie's hand. "I'm fine. This woman, whoever she is, saved me from some jerk at the truck stop last night. I can at least hear what she has to say."

Rox cut in. "That jerk might have been the serial killer."

Both cult sisters spun toward Rox and stared. After a moment, Ronnie laughed and shook her head. "More phony drama." She rolled her eyes at Emma, then walked out of the room.

Rox took another step toward Emma. "Please just come with me. It's only temporary. This place will still be here after your mother's gone." Rox had a flash of guilt for pushing that extreme emotional button. But she couldn't let Emma stay and ruin her own life. Or end up dead like Jolene. She just needed a few minutes alone with the girl.

"You'll bring me back here?" Emma asked with wide eyes.

"Of course." Rox heard a beep in her pocket. Was that Marty? Had ten minutes passed already? She didn't want to reach for her phone and break the moment. But she needed to let Marty know she was fine, so he didn't barge in and spook Emma. But if the entrance locked automatically—as a prison would—he probably couldn't get inside at all. Rox reached for Emma's arm and gently tugged her toward the swinging kitchen doors. As they walked through, she slipped her other hand into her pocket, feeling for her phone.

Across the empty cafeteria, the lobby door burst open, and Blackstone charged through. "What the fuck is going on?"

God damn it! Rox braced for trouble but kept moving. He wasn't armed, thank god. At least not that she could see. "Emma is coming with me to see her mother."

"Like hell she is." Blackstone lurched forward and grabbed the girl's other arm.

"Stop!" Emma shook them both off and backed away. "I want to call my mom." She held out her hand. "I need a cell phone."

Rox pulled out her burner phone to show she was willing. But she didn't want to give Emma the time to make the call. She had to keep this moving before shit got real.

"Don't believe a word this woman says." Blackstone used a military commander's voice, a man who expected his orders to be obeyed.

Rox's loathing threatened to derail her. She had to bite back several ugly comments.

"She lied to my father to get me out of here," Blackstone continued. "You can't trust her." He stepped toward Emma. "Tell her to go."

Emma's lips trembled.

Rox scrambled for a counter-argument. "Deacon Blackstone is a fraud. He's using the money he got from your mother to pay for his own father's care in a nursing home."

Emma's eyes widened. "I thought it was for veterans."

Blackstone started to respond, but Rox shouted over him. "Very little of the money he takes in goes to help people. I've seen the charity's books." *Another lie.* Rox kept rolling, surprised at her own guile. "He also might have killed Bethany. She was going to leave the cult and take her monthly royalties with her."

Emma's mouth dropped open, then snapped shut. "That can't be true. Any of it." The girl turned to Blackstone.

He was already pleading with her. "Lies, all lies. You know me. You know the work we do. The police questioned me about Bethany and cleared me." Blackstone spun toward Rox. "Get the fuck out!"

The power of his voice visibly alarmed Emma, and she started to cry. "I'm so confused."

Rox spoke with a gentle voice. "He recruits girls with guilt. Girls who hate themselves and are easy to manipulate. He goes after girls whose families have money." She moved toward Emma, locking eyes with her. "Deacon Blackstone only cares about himself and living the good life—using other people's guilt and money." Rox had planned to say all this in the car after they left, but this was her chance.

Something clicked in Emma's eyes, and she reached out and grabbed Rox's arm. "Take me to my mother, please."

Hell yes! Rox grabbed the girl's hand, spun, and strode toward the door.

Blackstone followed, still pleading. "Emma, you need to trust me. You know we feed people at the soup kitchen. What we do here is real and meaningful."

Rox kept moving, and Emma stayed with her, not looking at Blackstone or responding to him. He kept pace, pleading as they walked. In the lobby, he shouted, "When you realize this bitch is lying to you, remember that I'll take you back."

Out of the corner of her eye, Rox watched him storm down the hall, enter another room, and slam the door. She pushed on the bar handle of the main door, keeping a grip on Emma, and they stepped out into the bright sun.

Marty stood a foot away, his hand under his jacket. "Thank god. I was about to go around back and break a window." He shook his head. "Sorry, but Blackstone slammed in here and got inside before I could stop him. I was trying to warn you."

"It's okay. Let's go."

"Who is he?" Emma tensed and pulled away from Rox, her expression fearful now.

A car roared into the parking area, and they all looked over. Margo's minivan.

Rox tensed. *Damn!* This was supposed to be done. She turned to Emma. "He's my partner. He's here to help. Please get in the car."

The minivan slammed to a stop five feet from them. Margo jumped out, pointed a handgun, and shouted at her and Marty. "Get off this property!"

Oh fuck. Rox instinctively glanced at her stepdad, mentally willing him to keep his gun out of sight. But he was a retired cop, and his Glock was already drawn.

"Emma's coming with us." Marty sounded calm.

Abruptly Margo grabbed Emma's arm and jerked her toward the red mini-van. "Get in, Emma."

"I want to see my mother," the girl cried out.

"I'll take you. Just get in my van. You can't trust these people."

What was Margo up to? Rox was flummoxed. This didn't make sense.

Emma rounded the front of the red vehicle and opened the passenger door on the other side.

Marty, who was closer, shouted, "No, Emma!" He rushed forward, as if to grab the girl.

A sharp blast rang out, and Marty went down.

No! Rox rushed to his aid, glancing up at the crazy woman to see if she would shoot again. Margo was getting into her vehicle.

"Damn it, Marty!" Rox kneeled down, pulling off her jacket to stop the blood gushing from his chest. "Where's the hole?"

"In my right pec, maybe my lung. Missed my heart." He grabbed her hand. "I'll be okay. Go after Emma." His speech was labored. "Margo isn't planning to take her home."

Rox heard the minivan tearing out of the driveway. She didn't think so either. "I'm not leaving you."

"You have to." Marty tried to sit up.

Rox pushed him back down, pressing her jacket against his wound. "Just stay quiet and minimize the bleeding."

"Roxanne, honey. I've been meaning to tell you something."

"Not now." She needed to call 911. Where the hell was her phone?

"I have a heart condition," Marty muttered. "It's gonna kill me. Maybe not for a couple years, but maybe next month." His voice was rough, the words catching as waves of pain hit him. "Either way, I have nothing to lose."

What? He hadn't even seemed sick. Was this a ploy to get her to go after Emma? No, the truth was on his face. A wave of grief rolled over her, and Rox couldn't think or speak.

The sound of footsteps broke through her paralysis, and Rox turned, braced for more conflict. A young freckled girl kneeled next to her. "I'm Skeeter. I can help." The girl pressed on Marty's wound. "I overhead everything, and I'm worried about Emma. Margo makes all the sisters sign a will that leaves everything to the charity."

What? Rox tried to process the possibilities. That meant the charity would inherit Bethany's royalties. But why was Margo taking Emma somewhere? Emma didn't have any money of her own . . . as long as her parents were alive.

Marty let out a grunt. "See? Emma's in danger. Go!"

Rox was torn. Marty needed a paramedic. *Shit.* Her phones were in her pockets. "I need my jacket for a second."

Skeeter lifted the jacket and a phone slipped out, landing on Marty's chest. Rox grabbed it, called 911, and reported the incident, giving only the basics and location. Her brain was functioning now, and she had a plan. She held her hand over the phone and turned to Skeeter. "Can you drive?"

"Of course."

"Great." Rox spoke again to the dispatcher. "We'll drive toward the Linnwood Care Facility and meet the ambulance." She hung up. "Let's get him in the car."

Marty sat up, and they grabbed him under his arms. "Ready?" Rox didn't expect an answer, but Skeeter said yes, still gripping the bloody jacket. Together they lifted Marty to his feet and helped him into the back of his sedan. "Keys?"

Lying down across the seat, Marty pulled them from his pocket, then pressed his hands over his wound. Rox handed the keys to Skeeter. "You drive. I'll get out down the road where my car is parked." She climbed into the passenger seat and looked over the back at Marty. "Don't even think about dying. Six months, two years, whatever you have left—I want every minute of it."

CHAPTER 29

Emma buckled herself in, afraid of how fast Margo was driving. She closed her eyes and leaned back in the seat, crying softly. Was Deacon a good guy or a con man? Was her mother dying or not? She didn't know who to trust or believe. This was all so weird and confusing. She looked over at Margo. The woman was obviously upset and focused on something important. The thought scared her even more, and she had to ask, "Why did you shoot that man?"

Margo shook her head, as if Emma had said something stupid. "He had a gun! They were abducting you!"

Were they? It hadn't seemed like it. The woman—what was her name? Jolene?—had helped her at the truck stop. But maybe Jolene had been there to abduct her that night too. Emma wasn't surprised to learn her parents had hired someone to bring her home. They thought money solved everything. But something weird was going on here, and it had to involve her mother. Why else would Margo be taking her home? She worked up the courage to ask, "Do you know if my mother is sick?"

Margo let out a harsh laugh. "As if I care." She snapped her head to look at Emma, her face contorted. "Do you know what that bitch did to me?"

Emma recoiled. Margo knew her mom? How? "Why did you call her a bitch?" She was so confused.

"She stole my boyfriend. My fiancé! We were engaged, and I was supposed to marry Dave. I was supposed to have the good life! And that cunt"—spit flew out of Margo's mouth—"who was supposed to be my best friend seduced him away from me."

Would her mother do that? Maybe. She liked to get what she wanted. "When did you know her? In high school?" Emma was still struggling to understand everything she'd heard, and Margo's hostility was scaring her.

"College too." Margo made a fast turn onto a new road.

Emma stared out the window, wondering where they were really going. "You're taking me home, right?"

"Of course." Margo gave her a nasty smile. "I don't want you at the property anymore. I'm tired of sharing Deacon with pretty young girls."

"But Deacon said you had an open relationship."

Another harsh laugh. "He is so full of shit. And you are so gullible. He only wanted your parents' money."

Emma cringed and broke into sobs. How could she have been so stupid? The last four months of her life now seemed like a cruel joke. And so did Margo's relationship. "Why do you stay with Deacon? And why do you guys even run the soup kitchen?"

"Oh, I'm done with Deacon. He just doesn't know it yet." Margo abruptly pulled off the road into a turnout with no house in sight.

A flash of fear shot through Emma's chest. "Why are we stopping?"

"I have a quick thing to take care of." Margo fumbled in her pocket, then turned to face her.

Emma saw the needle coming too late. Margo plunged it into her arm before she could even protest. The drug hit hard, and her body went weak. Emma tried to speak but couldn't form words. The last thing she saw was a big roll of silver duct tape.

CHAPTER 30

Margo glanced at the dumb blonde girl, now unconscious, and hoped Emma's parents would be as easy to handle. What she had in mind was unlike anything she'd ever done. Well, except for killing Bethany. But that had been recent and rather spontaneous. Sort of. She'd hated Bethany since Deacon started screwing her months ago. She'd also fantasized about killing other sisters Deacon seduced, but actually doing it—strangling the life out of Bethany—had been a whole new experience. Intense and exhilarating! So much bottled rage had come gushing out, it almost scared her.

But it was such an easy way to solve problems. Why hadn't she done it before? Like when Jenny stole Dave from her. She should have killed the bitch, then comforted Dave, and won him back. Her whole life would have been different. Ronnie's life would have been different. Margo let out a harsh sound, halfway between a laugh and a sob. Actually Ronnie wouldn't even exist. The baby she would have made with Dave would be like the sweet, easy girl slumped next to her—instead of the troubled, addicted, pain-in-the-ass kid Ronnie had been.

Margo glanced at Emma again. Spoiled little brat. A loud honk startled her, and Margo jerked her head back to the road. She had to calm herself, focus on driving, and mentally walk through her plan. This was her ticket out. Out of her disgusting job as a caregiver and all the damn back pain that went with it, out of the ugly, isolated concrete complex, and out of her fucked-up relationship with Deacon. Now it all depended on the Carsons keeping a pile of cash in the house, probably in a safe.

She was confident they would part with it to keep Emma from getting her head blown off. Margo really wanted to get her hands on all the money they had in the bank too. Maybe millions. Technically it would have belonged to her if Jenny hadn't stolen Dave. Could she really access it? She'd been obsessing about it for months, originally thinking she would kill the Carsons first, then after Emma inherited the money, snuff her. Maybe make it look like the serial killer—if he still hadn't been caught by then. But that was a long-term plan that required patience, and she'd run out. When those people had come to take Emma, Margo had seen all the money evaporating, and she'd panicked. But plan B should work just fine.

If the Carsons were all killed during a home invasion gone wrong, Emma's inheritance would go to the charity. On paper, which was where it counted, Margo was a Sister Love founder as well as its money manager. She could, and would, access it all and cut Deacon out. It might take years for the Carsons' fortune to work its way through probate and legal challenges, but in the meantime, she could live on the cash from their safe. Dave's fortune would eventually come to her. The money had been meant for her all along. Jenny had just hijacked it for a while, and now it was time to get it back. First she had to send the text.

A minute later, she pulled off at an empty roadside produce stand and looked through her purse for Emma's phone. She'd taken it from Deacon's office after she'd caught him getting ready to fuck the girl yesterday. Killing Bethany had rattled her, and she'd started escalating her escape plans, including putting the phone in her purse so she could try to extort another donation from the Carsons. Deacon had stashed the ten grand he'd squeezed from them and wouldn't fucking tell her where. The idiot was going to give it to the damn nursing home. Then today, when she saw those mercenaries, or whoever they were, taking Emma, Margo had panicked and known she had to act. Now or never.

She texted Jenny and Dave with the same message, which they would assume came from their daughter: *I'll be home soon. If you want me to stay, it's very important that you're both there. I have something to tell you.*

That should bring both parents to the house. This needed to go well. Monday afternoon wasn't ideal timing, but she had to make it work. She'd planned this for an evening later in the week, but then everything had gone to shit. She punched the Carsons' address into her GPS, popped another OxyContin for courage, and got back on the road.

Twenty minutes later, she pulled into the circular driveway and stared at the two-story stone house with towers on each end—like a fucking castle. Queen Jenny had spent her last day on the throne. God, this would feel good. She'd been plotting her revenge for two decades. At first, it had just been a fantasy, a way to process her grief and anger. Then her nightmare marriage to Bruce, the psychopath, had deepened her rage and made her bitter. It had also produced Ronnie, a difficult child who'd been hard to love. But Margo had tried. Even after escaping Bruce, she'd still struggled to pay bills and find peace of mind. Then she'd met Deacon, and he'd seemed like a savior at first, but after a few years, she'd sensed his boredom with her sexually, and nothing she'd tried had recaptured it. The charity had been her idea for bringing more cash into their lives, but she hadn't realized Deacon would use it as an opportunity to fuck skinny teenagers. He'd also insisted they actually run a soup kitchen to feed hungry vets. Stupid! She'd wanted nothing to do with it. Then Ronnie had come back into their lives and needed something to focus on.

Margo studied the scene. Only one car was in front of the house, but Jenny's was probably in the three-car garage. No gardeners or hired help in sight. She glanced around the rich neighborhood. Not a soul anywhere. No noise either. Just blue sky and sunshine for these people.

Emma made a moaning sound, and Margo glanced over. The girl was blinking her eyes. Good, semiconscious was perfect. Margo reached under the seat, so glad she'd started prepping for this days ago. She pulled on the ski mask she'd borrowed from Ronnie's drawer—whatever it was for—and a pair of high-wedge boots to make herself appear taller, like a man. The bulky black sweatshirt over jeans also looked masculine. Would Jenny or Dave recognize her voice? Twenty years had passed since either of them had talked to her, and Margo had smoked a lot of pot and cigarettes in the early years, leaving her voice an alto instead of a soprano. But it didn't matter; they wouldn't be alive to tell anyone if they did recognize her.

CHAPTER 31

Margo braced herself. The hardest part would be getting the girl into the house—while keeping one hand ready to grab the Luger tucked into her waistband. The silencer was already in place on the weapon, and the roll of duct tape was in the sweatshirt's big front pocket. In her mind, she'd been prepping for years, fantasizing about killing Jenny. She could pull this off. Margo glanced at the girl one more time. The ketamine probably wouldn't last much longer. An old memory flashed, and Margo smiled. She'd been reading Jenny's Facebook page—as she did regularly to see what the husband-stealing bitch was up to—and Jenny had hinted at some tragedy that would keep her offline for a while. Pleased and curious, Margo had searched news sites for days until she found an article about Emma's accident. The thought of luring Jenny's guilt-ridden daughter into the charity and using Emma to get back at her enemy had made Margo's heart leap with joy.

The only real challenge had been staying patient while they earned the girl's loyalty. But that had given Margo time to craft a plan. She and Deacon had discussed fraud-based, non-violent ideas for how to access the Carsons' money, but he didn't know about her personal grudge. She'd secretly plotted her own scheme, originally planning to share the money with Deacon. But fuck him. Now it was time to take back what was rightfully hers and get the hell out of this miserable, wet state.

Margo got out of the car and moved quickly to the other side. Emma's eyes were open, but she was still out of it. Margo pulled her out, then wrapped her left arm around the girl's waist, keeping her right hand free to grab the gun. "Start walking," she urged. Emma took a tentative step forward. "Just do it!" Margo kept her voice low but threatening.

Emma stumbled forward, and Margo hurried up the stone path, half dragging the girl, pulling in as much oxygen as she could. Emma was skinny, but it was still an effort to keep her up and moving. Margo touched the hood of Dave's BMW, and found the engine still warm. He'd come home in response to the text. Margo smiled. She was about to see him again in person for the first time in twenty years. She'd been following his life too, but he wasn't on Facebook, so she'd only had an occasional glimpse from outside his firm.

On the wide stone porch, Margo scanned the area around the ornate double door for a camera and didn't see one. It was probably hidden. But so was her face. Margo reached for the bronze door handle, hoping to get lucky and find it unlocked. The door pushed open. *Hot damn.* She wanted to surprise them. Voices from another room pulled her to the right, and she passed through a large dining area with fancy china cabinets.

Dave appeared in the arched opening to the kitchen. He was fatter, grayer, and older than she remembered—but still handsome. He started to speak, but stopped and simply inhaled sharply.

Margo looked around for someplace to dump the girl.

"Is Emma all right? Did you hurt her?" Dave's voice was tight with fear.

Before Margo could answer, Jenny burst into the room. "What's going on?"

Tired of the weight, Margo let Emma drop to the tile floor. The girl cried out, sounding more awake.

"Oh my god!" Jenny rushed toward her daughter.

Margo pulled out her Luger and shouted, "Stop!" She stepped between Jenny and the prone girl with duct-taped wrists. "If you want your daughter to live, you will do exactly as I say." Margo pitched her voice as low as she could. "Walk backward into the kitchen. I want to see your hands at all times." This room had tall windows with gauzy, see-through curtains, and she needed more privacy.

The Carsons backed slowly through the archway, their eyes glancing between the gun and their daughter. Margo followed, dragging the semiconscious girl with her. Inside the massive kitchen, a table stood in the breakfast nook to the right and a counter with bar stools separated the space from the cooking area. The nook had a window too, so she gestured for Dave to move left. "Empty your pockets, then sit on the end bar stool."

"What do you want?" Dave pleaded as he put his phone and wallet on the granite counter. "Just tell me, and I'll give it to you. Please leave Emma alone."

Margo wanted to instill more fear, so she didn't answer. She reached into her pocket for the duct tape and handed it to Jenny. "Tape his wrists, then tape him to the chair."

Jenny stared, open-mouthed. "I don't know how to do that."

Oh fuck. "Are you stupid? Just do it, or I'll shoot Emma."

"No!" Tears running down her face, Jenny started to tape her husband's wrists.

Her stolen husband. Margo sized up her old enemy. Pudgy in her gut and hips, but her hair was still a beautiful blonde, and her face looked good. But Jenny could afford to take care of her skin and get those little cosmetic tune-ups that kept rich women from looking their age. *Narcissistic bitch.*

Margo stepped closer to inspect the wrist tape on Dave. It was too loose, but it didn't matter. These people would be dead soon. She just had to make it look like a random home invasion gone wrong. Which it was, except for the random part. "Tape him to the chair and make it tight."

Jenny fumbled her way through the binding process as Dave asked, "Why do you have Emma? Are you with the Sister Love cult?"

They weren't a cult! Margo had to bite her tongue to keep from arguing. Instead she said, "I found this girl wandering along the road. Just your lucky day." She gestured at Jenny. "Tape his mouth too."

When the bitch was done, Margo pointed the Luger at her. "I want all the cash you have in the house. Open the safe. Or safes. I'm coming with you."

Jenny looked at Dave, and he nodded.

Suddenly Emma called out, "Mom!"

Jenny started toward her daughter, but Margo caught her arm. "Tape her mouth too. Quickly!"

As she stuck a piece of tape over her daughter's lips, the mother whispered, "Sorry."

Margo jerked Jenny to her feet. "Let's get the cash!"

"The safe is upstairs," Jenny said, her voice breaking.

Together, they moved through the arch. As they passed the crying girl, Margo threatened, "Stay quiet, both of you, or everyone dies."

Jenny hustled up a wide set of stairs, and Margo followed. So far, this was going well. She was minutes away from holding a stack of cash that would take her to Arizona and her new life. One without cheating Deacon or her butt-wiping job. She didn't even plan to take Ronnie. She was done with everyone.

Jenny led her into a plush master bedroom, decorated in shades of pale mint and peach. Envy filled Margo's body, as if someone had poured poison down her throat. Jenny didn't deserve this room, and Margo couldn't wait to end her spoiled life, maybe right here. "Hurry!"

Jenny ran to a big landscape painting and pulled it down. The woman's hands shook as she turned the knob on the safe, and she had to start over. When the thick metal door opened and Margo spotted the stacks of cash, her heart skipped a beat. *Fuck yes!* This would buy her a nice apartment in Tucson with a view of the mountains. She looked around for something to put everything in, yanked a pillow off the bed, and removed the case. "Load it all into this. The jewelry too." She handed Jenny the pale-green pillowcase.

"Not my mother's ring, please," Jenny begged.

Margo laughed. "All of it. Even those papers." She thought they might be stock certificates or something that had value.

While Jenny transferred the goods, Margo couldn't resist saying, "How does it feel to have *your* life stolen?"

The other woman's lips trembled. "What are you talking about?"

"Dave, the fiancé you stole from me."

For a long moment, Jenny was silent, her eyes flashing as she tried to make the connection. "Margaret?"

Margo grabbed the loaded pillowcase. "Payback time." She wanted to shoot the bitch right here in her precious mint-and-peach bedroom. But it would be better to kill them all at once, so she could get the hell out immediately after. That way, she could make Jenny watch her daughter and husband die first. *Yeah*. She liked that idea. "Downstairs!"

CHAPTER 32

Rox squeezed Marty's hand one last time, then jumped out of his car and ran to hers. The cult girl behind the wheel of Marty's car waited, so Rox pulled out first, throwing dirt as she raced out of the logging road's entrance. Margo was long gone, so this effort could be a fool's errand. Margo had claimed she was taking Emma home, and Rox had doubted it at the time. But Skeeter's revelation played over in her head. Margo had made the members sign wills leaving everything to the charity. If Margo was desperate—and shooting Marty had definitely seemed like an act of desperation—all of the Carsons could be in danger.

Or not. Maybe Margo had just been protecting Emma. Rox and Marty had been trespassing, and Marty had pulled his weapon. A grand jury probably wouldn't even indict Margo for the shooting. What the crazy woman planned to do next was the real issue. Maybe she was just taking Emma home. Rox couldn't convince herself of that. She put in her earpiece and called Kyle. As the phone rang, she silently begged him to pick up.

On the fifth ring, he did. "This isn't a good time, Rox. Can I call you back?"

"No. Something could be going down. My clients' daughter is in a car with an armed woman who just shot Marty."

"What the hell? Where are you?"

"On Barton Road, a couple miles from Deacon Blackstone's work camp. But I'm headed toward my clients' home." Why was she still being discreet?

"Is Marty okay?"

"Yes. It's a shoulder wound, and one of the cult members is taking him to meet the ambulance."

"You were doing an extraction? Trespassing?"

Would this call come back to bite her in the ass? Maybe. But if the Carsons were in danger, she needed help. "Sort of, but something else might be happening now, and I'm not sure what it is."

"You'll have to be more explicit." He sounded intrigued but impatient.

"After the shooting, Margo, the other cult founder, told Emma to get in her car and that she would take her home. Then they took off. But I think Emma might be in danger." That sounded like she was making a huge deal out of nothing.

"Why danger? Did she threaten the girl?" His impatience had worsened.

"No, but all the girls in the cult have signed wills leaving everything to the charity."

A long silence. "So Bethany's royalties now belong to the charity?"

"Most likely." Rox saw the junction ahead and pressed the brakes. She'd been hitting seventy.

Kyle sighed. "This development is interesting, but it doesn't sound like an immediate situation. I have a brief meeting now, then I'll call you back and we can talk through this."

So no backup from Kyle. She should have expected it. Rox made the turn, still thinking. Based on such weak information, would a dispatcher even send a patrol cop to the Carsons' house? Doubtful.

"Rox?"

She decided to give Kyle more detail and rattled off her clients' address in Lake Oswego, only about twenty minutes away. "If you can't reach me after your meeting, send a patrol unit there, okay?"

A slight hesitation. "Sure."

Rox hung up, disappointed, even though she wasn't sure what she'd expected. Regardless of how benign the situation sounded, she'd seen the look in Margo's eyes. The woman was on a mission—and armed. Rox pressed the accelerator.

The drive took less time than she'd expected, with light traffic on a Monday afternoon and her pushing the limits of safety. Two cars were in the driveway at the Carson home. A silver BMW that probably belonged to Dave and Margo's minivan. Both were empty. Where was Jenny? Rox climbed out, noticing the three-car garage.

With a ten-minute head start, Margo had been inside the house for at least a few minutes. That seemed odd—why would the Carsons welcome her?—but not alarming by itself. Dave being home in the middle of the day was also peculiar. He hadn't been willing to leave work long enough to see Emma for an hour Friday afternoon, so what was he doing here now? A thought hit her, and Rox was embarrassed by her call to Kyle. Margo was probably in there soliciting another donation. That's what charities did. And Sister Love probably saw the Carsons as a soft target. Rox worried that she wouldn't get credit for the extraction now. She'd done everything but drive Emma to safety. But if the Carsons refused to pay her the bonus, there was nothing she could do. They didn't even know her real name.

Rox needed to be sure Emma had made it home. She climbed out of her car and started toward the front of the house. A shiver ran up her spine. This felt like the time she'd done a domestic call during her patrol cop days, the most dangerous call-out. Only then, she'd been armed. *Damn.* Reluctantly she turned back, unlocked her car, and slipped her Glock into her waistband. The worst place to carry it, but she wasn't wearing a holster, and it wasn't a pocket gun.

At the door, she started to knock, but a popping sound startled her. Was that muted gunfire? Her pulse jumped. The sound had come from deep inside the house. A muffled cry, then sobbing followed. Rox pushed open the door and hurried inside. The spacious living room was empty, but she heard talking in the area to her right. Rox scooted across the dining room and braced against the wall next to the arched opening. She peered around the edge, spotting Emma on the kitchen floor with her hands and mouth duct taped. A person in a ski mask paced back and forth, gun in hand. *Fuck!* Was that Margo? The petite size and shape sort of matched the woman who'd just shot Marty. Beyond the intruder, Dave Carson was duct taped to a bar stool, slumped forward and bleeding from his belly. Jenny Carson was next to him, unrestrained and sobbing. Rox noticed the assailant holding a pillowcase that looked half full of small items. This was a robbery!

Rox eased out her Glock, a tremor in her arm. She wasn't ready for this!

"How does that feel, Jenny?" the assailant mocked. "To have Dave taken from you?" The voice was Margo's, but it sounded low and muffled through the ski mask.

Jenny looked at Margo with terror in her eyes. "I'm so sorry! But that was twenty years ago! Just take the cash and go. Leave us alone."

Twenty years ago?

Margo laughed, a weird, raspy sound. "Oh, I will. But you're all going to die first, and I'm going to watch you suffer."

No! She couldn't let that happen. Cop mode kicked in, and Rox stepped out from the wall and spun into the opening. "Put the gun down!"

The assailant turned and lifted her handgun. Rox started to call out Margo's name, as her training had taught her, but she held back. Maybe Margo would just run out of the house with the loot and drive away. *Please!*

Instead, Margo turned to the girl on the floor and pointed her gun. Emma was sitting up now, her eyes wide with fear.

Damn! "Put the gun down!" Rox shouted. "I will shoot!" She pulled her other hand up to steady the Glock.

Margo glanced her way, then took a step toward Emma and laughed.

Jenny screamed.

Rox pulled the trigger, the sound deafening. The masked woman staggered back and fell against the countertop, smacking her head. She slumped onto the floor, bleeding from her shoulder. The gun landed in her lap with her hand still around it, but the intruder wasn't moving. Rox grabbed the weapon and slid it across the dining room floor. She didn't want it in her pocket and couldn't hold both weapons. She kneeled down and reached for the mask. Black with a red band around the neck. *What?* The assailant at the truck stop had worn the same mask. Rox yanked it off, and Margo stared blankly at her. Was she the serial killer? Rox remembered the rest of the scene at the truck stop. The attacker had been several inches taller than Margo, and the car had been small, boxy, and bluish—unlike the minivan Margo drove. Wait, Rox had seen a vehicle like that somewhere recently. The work camp . . . Ronnie's car! Dear god, were the mother and daughter both crazy?

While Emma cried and Jenny tried to hold back her husband's blood, Rox pulled out her cell phone and called 911.

CHAPTER 33

Tuesday, April 25, 5:00 p.m.

Rox stepped into the room and braced for seeing Marty in a hospital bed. All those years as a cop, and this was the first time he'd ended up here. But he was sitting up in a chair by the bed and looked pretty normal except for the loose pale-print gown.

"Hey, how are you feeling?"

"Irritable. They won't let me eat, and I hate watching TV that isn't recorded."

He sounded so good. Not weak or impaired at all. Her worry melted away. "When are you getting out of here?"

"I'm leaving tomorrow morning, come hell or high water. So you might as well bring my pants."

Rox laughed. "Will do." She pulled up a chair beside him.

"Do you have an update for me? Like what the hell was going on with that crazy Margo?"

"Not yet. I'm having dinner with Kyle soon and should know more after that." She'd visited Marty briefly last evening after spending hours at the police department being questioned. But he'd been so out of it, he probably didn't remember what she'd told him about the incident at the Carsons'. *Incident!* Three people had been shot yesterday afternoon, and she'd fired the third bullet. Margo had died of the trauma to her head, but Dave Carson was alive and down the hall. She would visit him briefly too. But not yet. "So what's the deal with your heart?" she asked.

Marty let out a small sigh. "It's a defective valve they can't fix. It could give out tomorrow or not for another couple of years."

She refused to accept that. "Medical breakthroughs happen all the time. Let's keep looking for new doctors and new surgeries to try."

He was quiet for a moment, then laughed. "I'm glad you're still stubborn. I am too. I won't give up without a fight."

"You'd better not."

"And I'm still taking care of business. Your problem with Cubano is over. He's not likely to ever threaten you again." He looked pleased with himself.

"What did you do?"

"Let's just say I arranged for his arrest." He gave a little wink. "And he will be convicted."

Rox didn't want to know the details. "Thanks." She tried to think of what else to talk about. She still wasn't good at chitchat, even with Marty. "So, tell me about your girlfriend."

"There's not much to say. Her name is Grace, and I met her swing dancing like you guessed."

"You getting busy with her yet?"

He blushed. "None of your business."

Rox laughed. "I thought so. Hey, I should go see my client, then meet Kyle for dinner." She stood to leave.

"Call me with the case details even if it's late. I can't sleep in here anyway."

"Will do."

Rox headed down the hall, looking for the number Jenny Carson had given her. She found it at the end, a big private room—no surprise. The door was open though, so she called out, "Hello," and walked in. Jenny sat in a chair by the hospital bed, and Emma lay on the visitor lounger near the window. She jumped up when she saw Rox.

Silently the girl rushed over and squeezed her in a big hug. Surprised, Rox placed her hands on Emma's back. She'd never been much of a hugger, except with boyfriends.

"Thank you! I know they paid you to help me, but still, you saved my life twice!"

"You're welcome." Rox wanted to give Emma words of encouragement but decided to let the specialists handle it.

Jenny came over and hugged her briefly too. "You'll always be special to this family. If you ever need anything, please, let us know."

"I appreciate that." All she really needed now was to get paid. "Let me take a photo of you and Emma for the bank." She snapped a picture with her phone, realizing all these precautions were pointless now that her clients had seen her face. "I wish your family the best." Rox, feeling uncomfortable with all the emotion, glanced at Mr. Carson, who was sleeping. "Is he doing all right?"

"Yes. He'll make a full recovery."

"Good news." Rox smiled and turned to leave.

Mrs. Carson called out, "Wait, please." Rox turned back, confused, and Jenny handed her a satchel. "This is to double your bonus. You earned it. And if your partner has medical expenses not covered by insurance, we'll take care of them."

"Thank you!" Rox wanted to ask about Margo's twenty-year grudge over a stolen boyfriend but didn't. The Carsons had been through enough. "I have to go." She turned to Emma. "Take care of yourself."

Emma nodded. "I'll try."

Rox hurried out.

Kyle was ten minutes late for their dinner date, but Rox was so eager to get an update on the Sister Love charity she didn't even comment when he sat down. She gave him a minute to settle in and order a beer before she peppered him with questions. "Did you search the work camp? Did you arrest Deacon Blackstone?"

"Yes, and we charged him with assault and some other minor bullshit, but if he makes bail, we can't hold him." Kyle patted her hand, then pulled back. "Don't worry, we're still investigating and talking to other cult members. Also, fraud detectives are looking closely at the charity's financials."

Rox laughed. "I know this is petty, but I called the IRS and asked them to audit the charity's books."

Kyle laughed too. "Remind me to never piss you off."

The waiter arrived, and they ordered dinner before Rox started in again. "What about Ronnie Preston? Did you check out my theory that she might be the I-5 Killer?"

"We have her in custody too." Kyle leaned in and lowered his voice. "The tread marks on her Toyota match the evidence from the first victim, and we found three locks of different hair in a jewelry-box-type thing in her bedroom. We suspect it's trophy hair from the murders, but we won't have the DNA results for weeks." Kyle shook his head. "What a hornet's nest of crazies!"

No kidding! "Ronnie sounds like a real psychopath!" An image of Margo wielding a gun flashed in Rox's brain. "Her mother probably is too." Margo's death had bothered her at the time, but now Rox felt mostly numb about it. The crazy woman had been about to kill three innocent people over a stolen boyfriend two decades earlier. Well, that plus twenty-five thousand in cash and jewels.

Kyle had more to report. "They found bottles of OxyContin in Margo's luggage. They all had other people's names. It looks like she was stealing pain pills from patients at the hospital."

"An opioid addiction might partially explain why she snapped, but I wonder what other crimes she's committed over the years and gotten away with."

Kyle leaned in again. "She may have killed Bethany. The tire marks at that scene were different from the others, and so was the pressure on the victim's neck. But we don't have forensic results from Margo's car yet. The techs are still processing her personal items."

Something he'd said a moment earlier clicked. "That would explain why you found only three locks of hair in Ronnie's collection, instead of four."

"That's what we're thinking." Kyle gave a sheepish grin. "The neighborhood boy you located? He admitted seeing Margo drive by soon after Bethany left his house. Margo probably picked up the girl and strangled her on her way to work. The body's dump site was just off her route by a few miles."

"The task force has been busy!"

"The sergeant pulled everyone off other leads to focus on the freaks at the Sister Love complex. It's been a treasure trove. Unfortunately Ronnie hasn't told us anything, but we'll keep questioning her until she does."

Rox mulled over the mother-daughter murders. "Margo probably killed Bethany for the royalty money, then went after the Carsons for their money. But I wonder what the hell motivated Ronnie. I mean, other than the desire to kill."

"Jealousy of younger, prettier girls? No daddy love? We may never know."

"I wonder how she met them and targeted them."

Kyle sipped his beer before responding. "Now that we have her in custody, we've looked at Ronnie's cell phone and mapped her mobility. She frequented neighborhoods with shelters for runaway teens."

"A family of predators!"

Their food came, and over dinner, they talked about the Sister Love group and how young women fell prey to such scams. But after a while, Rox had to change the subject. Jolene was never far from her mind.

"Did the Carsons pay your bonus fee?" Kyle asked.

"They doubled it." It still made her grin.

It was his turn to ask questions. "Are they getting their daughter some counseling? We need her to testify."

"They have a deprogramming specialist staying at the house. Emma will get the best care money can buy." The other Sister Love members might end up on the streets, but Rox had called several women's support groups and asked them to help. It was all she could do. Emotion filling her heart, Rox reached over to hold Kyle's hand for a moment.

He gently pulled away. "Rox, we have to talk about something."

That didn't sound good. "What is it?"

"Your treatments. They've changed you. And I'm not sure it's working for me."

She'd known this was coming. "I'm sorry to hear that. I'm not sure about the treatments either, but I think I owe it to myself to continue and see where I end up. They've already made me a better investigator."

"Because you're more deceptive?"

That hurt. "Not fair. It's just a job thing. You do it too."

He was quiet for a long moment. "You're more affectionate too."

"So?"

"But that's not us. We've had an unspoken agreement."

Rox was quiet. She hadn't been completely sure after the second session that she would actually continue the treatments, but she was now. She hoped they might even help her get over her own guilt about Jolene. She'd been trapped by it, similar to the way the Sister Love girls had been. She needed to move on.

"I like the new me, and I plan to keep my appointment tomorrow. I want to be better at this extraction business, because there are more people who need my help." She thought about Marty, and how great he'd been to her all her life. She felt like she'd cheated him by not being fully emotionally engaged, even though it wasn't her fault. "I want to be the kind of person who notices what other people are thinking and feeling." She gave Kyle a sad smile. "The effect probably won't last. Should I look you up when it wears off?"

He smiled back, looking equally sad. "Sure. I'd like that."

She thought of one more thing. "I also want to wear something besides blue." She pushed aside her napkin and stood up. "But it will never be pink."

On her way out of the restaurant, her burner phone rang, and she answered it. "Karina Jones. How can I help you?"

ABOUT THE AUTHOR

L.J. Sellers writes the bestselling Detective Jackson mystery/thriller series—a five-time winner of the Readers' Favorite Awards. She also pens the high-octane Agent Dallas series and provocative stand-alone thrillers. Her twenty novels have been praised by reviewers, and she's one of the highest-rated crime-fiction authors on Amazon.

L.J. resides in Eugene, Oregon, where many of her novels are set, and she's an award-winning journalist who earned the Grand Neal Award for editorial excellence in business publications. When not plotting murders, she enjoys stand-up comedy, cycling, and zip-lining. She's also been known to jump out of airplanes.